THE COSMIC BUNGLERS

By
GEOFF ST. REYNARD

I0616969

ARMCHAIR FICTION
PO Box 4369, Medford, Oregon   97501-0168

*For more information about Armchair Books and products, visit our
website at…*

www.armchairfiction.com

Or email us at…

armchairfiction@yahoo.com

AN INVASION FROM THE PAST?

It seemed impossible, but what other explanation was there for the sudden appearance of over a thousand 17th Century highwaymen, seemingly plopped down in the middle of the southwestern desert of the United States? But it was true. Everyday American travelers, coasting through the hot desert sands in their modern automobiles, were suddenly being dry-gulched and robbed by ancient-looking hoodlums on horseback.

But what connection did it all have to a top secret experiment involving man's first attempt at surpassing the speed of light? Was it time travel, or was it something else?

FOR A COMPLETE SECOND NOVEL, TURN TO PAGE 83

CAST OF CHARACTERS

SAM BLACK

He was a fuel expert for a tiny new flying ship. Its top speed? In excess of the speed of light!

BARBARY

Probably the most beautiful woman Sam Black had ever seen. But she was just a common street wench, circa 1725!

PETE ASHTON

Sam's pal and fellow fuel expert—and without his help Sam's life wasn't worth a plugged nickel.

GALLOPING JONAS

This grandiose highwayman thought he was going to be the king of the world. Unfortunately for him he was in the wrong world.

KEMP

They would all soon owe him their lives, primarily because of his ability to handle a Thompson sub-machine gun!

GRANVILLE

Standing on top of a jeep at the head of a military charge isn't always the smartest thing you can do.

CHAPTER ONE

THE day we broke the light barrier was the day the highwaymen came back. The juxtaposition of Project Pow's successful inauguration with Galloping Jonas's holdup of the trans-continental bus was so perfect that we all drew the wrong conclusions... Let me tell it from the start.

Out on the Nevada desert there was a testing ground that was twenty miles long and as flat as an ivory chessboard. Flatter. It was sixty yards broad and at the center, ten full miles from either end, it was troughed pretty deeply, to compensate for the earth's curvature. Here is how totally *flat* it was; if you'd fired a bullet straight along its course at a height of half an inch from the concreted flooring, supposing that slug didn't waver, it would have ended half an inch above the floor twenty miles off. There'd never been anything in this world so flat and long before. I know. I helped to dig that fabulous trench.

I'd jockeyed a bulldozer three summers before going to the university. When I'd added an M. Sc., to my name— Sam Black, M. Sc., and not Samuel, dammit, I was christened Sam—I threw a nervous breakdown; too many books, too little play. The medics told me to do some labor with my big skinny hands, to forget fuels and ignore space stations. So instead of engineering the big ditch, I dozed part of it. Sweated and drank beer and listened to jazz, gradually knitting up the raveled nerve ends.

We finished the super-flat furrow and by then I'd toughened up and eased down to normal; which is why I'm alive, I suppose. One ounce less muscle on my six-three, 200-pound carcass, and I'd be lying in the weeds with Gothic Beall's dirk in my guts. I'll get to that.

I'm skipping around. Never wrote much except formulae and post cards before. Bear with me.

Then I went to my proper work, which was concerned with the incredible fuel we were utilizing on Project Pow. *Pow*—that was collegiate-style humor, that name, whistling in a dark that was full of impossible certainties and liable to explode all over us and end everything in a shower of sundered atoms. Project Pow was something we hadn't expected to accomplish for at least four hundred years. Not even a landing on the moon yet, and here we were with two freak discoveries that would enable us to surpass the speed of light.

The fuel was first—basic principle discovered in Oakland, California, last August. On its heels, in October, the invention of the new alloy sclerium—in a tiny laboratory in Quebec. We put the two together and got a missile that no speed could damage, powered with a fuel so powerful the mind boggled at its terrifying potential. So we'd built our flatland in the desert, and were ready to try it out.

Light travels, speaking in round figures, at a speed of 186,273 miles per second in air, and 186,320 in a vacuum. Our 20-mile trench was equipped with instruments that would give us the speed of an object in millionths of a second. We constructed a minuscule spaceship, and into its bowels we lowered an amount of calefite—the new fuel—that you could have mislaid on the point of a needle. At the north end of the ditch we erected our launching platform, spending eighteen days in the sighting of it. Down at the south end was a cradle contraption, which would snatch the preposterous toy out of the air at the end of its flight. Then we were ready to test.

For longer than I like to admit—our fearful procrastination seems cowardly now, in hind-sight—we hemmed and hawed, rechecking figures, calculating anew... Well, I remember when I was in grammar school and they were just about to break through the sound barrier, and a lot of intelligent men were scared stiff for fear the whole fabric of our planet would tear asunder. How infinitely vaster were the horrors of ignorant man, about to surpass the greatest velocity known—that of light itself! No one could predict what in the hell would happen.

IF we'd speculated for a decade we could never have predicted Galloping Jonas. A nova, sure. A system-wide cataclysm. Even if we'd thought of Time as a dimension, a dinosaur or a man from the twenty-ninth century. But not, heaven help us, Galloping Jonas and his good nag Tess!

Finally we brought ourselves to the point of desperation, of having to find out, and against the scree-ches of calamity-howlers all over the globe, we gathered one morning at the ditch and sent off our miniature ship.

The instruments measured its time of flight at just under a hundred and five millionths of a second, or somewhere in the neighborhood of 190,000 miles per second. Considerably brisker than light had that little scrap of sclerium flown, and the world, so far as we could tell, was still in little danger of exploding. There had been noise, certainly—a crash that brought echoes like machine-gun fire reverberating from the flat—but beyond a few windows shattered there was no damage.

The ship was examined, after it had cooled, and our belief in its indestructibility was confirmed. Then, as the awestruck congratulations were being passed around, someone, I forget who, suggested that maybe we didn't have a faster-than-light deal at all. The properties of calefite were only dimly understood. Mightn't it be that we had a medium of near-instantaneous teleportation here, instead of a super-fuel?

It shows how taut and distracted we were, that we believed this might be true. Nobody asked why the ship would have been teleported right down to the cradle rather than to Australia or Mars. We set up the experiment again and this time erected an enormous sheet of oiled paper at the trench's midpoint. Then we gave our toy its second flight. The heavy paper we picked up in shreds and patches all over the surrounding acre. The ship rested in the cradle, having once more exceeded light's speed limit, this time at roughly 189,240 m.p.s. Teleportation was out.

So twice in a single day, once at 9:46 a.m. and again at 3:16 p.m., we had broken the light barrier.

I think the newspaper report of the next incident tells it better than I could…

"June 3: At a point in the Mormon Range between Caliente and Mesquite, Nevada, at about ten o'clock tonight, a transcontinental bus of the Blackbird Lines was ambushed and robbed by a man who is being spoken of as a lunatic, a phantom, or a fantastically elaborate practical joker. Any of these guesses seems as good as the others.

"The driver, Bernard John, 28, told this reporter: 'I was rounding this bend and all of a sudden there was this big mess of brush and logs in the road and I had to stop the crate quick. Just as I opened the door there was a crash and down off the hill came this big black horse with the crackpot on top. He leaned in and shoved a couple of cannons into my face. They must have had three-inch bores in them. He was dressed like nothing you ever saw and I didn't understand one word in six he yelled at me, but I took it he was sticking up the bus and I didn't argue. Maybe I should have hit him with a spanner? I'm paid to be a hero?'

"The horseman dismounted and walked through the bus, collecting jewelry and money. No one made any move to attack him. He peered closely at the money, seeming astonished at it, though no one could tell why. He then returned to his horse, and after a long gaze at the front of the bus, he scratched his head, said 'Where did the nags go?' quite audibly, and galloped off down the highway.

"The following statement was taken by this reporter from Dr. H. Lloyd Rawlins, well-known historian, a passenger on the bus: 'My period is the early 18th Century. Save that the man's weapons and clothing were nearly new, he might have stepped directly out of Walpole's England. He was fair and well-built, six feet one or two, and spoke with a Norfolk accent in the idiom of 1725. He wore a cherry-black velvet coat with long skirts, a white silk waistcoat damasked in floral patterns, black velvet smallclothes, a burst of Flemish lace at the throat, opal stickpin, black leather boots, a cocked silver-fretted black satin hat, horseman's cloak and a long foppish black wig. There was a beautiful horn-gripped saber in his sword-belt and he carried a brace of silver-mounted horse pistols. When he examined the coins I gave him, he said, "Not a goblin or stag among 'em!" Those are old thieves' words for sovereign and shilling. I have no theory to offer at this time concerning the man.'

"The state police are alerted and an arrest is expected soon."

We read this item over coffee the next morning. We didn't connect it with our projectile out in the big ditch. We didn't do that for a week. And what we deduced was all wrong even then.

CHAPTER TWO

ON the tenth of June, after a week more or less quiet, the highwaymen struck in force. In Arizona, along the hot highways of New Mexico and Nevada, in Utah and as far as California's eastern borders, from dusk till sunup the fantastic bushrangers on their splendid big stallions thundered out of darkness to stop and rob cars, busses, and in one case, a freight train. Their tactics were usually to pile brush or logs across a stretch of deserted road. Their clothes and weapons were of antique pattern. Their take was generally small; and their expressions were invariably astounded.

"If it's a practical joke," said Pete Ashton, my sidekick and fellow fuel-man, looking up from the morning paper, "it's the most expensive one of all time. Did you read this thing?"

"Huh-uh."

"It estimates the number of men involved at more than eight hundred. Plus a horse for each one. Plus maybe fifteen hundred bucks' worth of costume apiece, and God knows how much for the pistols and swords."

"Hollywood," I hazarded. "Publicity stunt. Big new 4-D—not 3-D mind you—picture, Rock Brandon in *Forever Ethelberta...*"

"Won't hold water. Two men were shot when they objected to being hijacked. Both in critical condition. And think of the lawsuits! Federal government would send up half of Beverly Hills for twenty years." He leveled his gray eyes at me and got that little crease between them that means he's deadly serious. "Look here, Sam, has it occurred to you that possibly, just possibly, we're to blame?"

I caught his idea at once. It was one of those improbable moments when one of us had an idea and with half a dozen words conveyed it to the other in all its intricate, screwball complexity. There wasn't any need to amplify, but just to make some noise while I mulled it over. I said, "You mean we cracked a hole in Time? Reached back two and a half centuries and made a bridge over which these desperate gentry came riding? That what you mean, Verne?"

"That's what I mean, Wells."

"But Burroughs, old chap, you're talking through your space warp." I didn't think he was, but I had to banter and chaff while I looked at the enormous and chaotic contingencies.

"Like hell I am, H. Rider. Free your mind of those yokelish prejudices and listen. Item: although some of the highwaymen are dressed in new clothes, others wear rags at least twenty years old. Where would they have found paduasoy and velvet jackets that old? Has some eccentric millionaire been planning this for decades?"

"Maybe. Go on."

"Item: nearly all of them expressed wonder at the horseless carriages, and plenty of witnesses swear it was genuine. Item: our currency baffles 'em—truly bewilders 'em, and you can't tell me there are 800 actors good enough to put across a phony surprise at something as common as money."

"It ain't common enough for me," I said. Down at the base of my neck the short hairs were bristling with cold dawning fear of what we might have done.

"Last item that I can think of: that historian, what's-his-name, says that the Norfolk 18th-Century accent could not have been reproduced by anyone other than a handful of specialists. Period. End of theory. I just may be sick all over the waffles."

"I wish," I said slowly, "I wish there was somebody else here to talk it over with. I don't wholly trust our opinions, Pete—never have since we invented that super-octane gas in chem class our freshman year. It turned out to be lemonade. Remember? We are inclined to go off deep ends with some regularity…"

"I'm not suggesting that we can do a damn thing but talk about it, even if it is true," he said. "We broke the light barrier and whatever's done is done. I'm not going to commit suicide over the thing. I simply say it was probably us and our blasted fuel and our bloody sclerium that warped, tore, bridged, or scrambled the fourth dimension. Time, all to hell, I wish they all hadn't flown to Washington to explain what we did to our beloved Congress. Hang it, there won't be anybody here but soldiers and laborers for a week. What we need is some giant brain to try this on. We may be mole-hilling like crazy."

"Try the telephone," I said suddenly. "Half the gang are at the same hotel, the Hilstone, and you can get a multi-connection and see what they all think of it. I'll see if the radio has any late news while you talk to 'em."

"You were always the practical one," said Pete admiringly, "while I was the young, tousle-headed dreamer, handsome but awfully ineffectual. Phone it is."

And it was in this way that we discovered that neither the telephone nor the radio was working.

We took them both apart and put them together and couldn't get a murmur out of them, and we swore and sweated in the desert heat, and not once did it occur to us to connect the failure of our communication instruments with the appearance in the American West of eight hundred Georgian gentlemen of the high road.

CHAPTER THREE

ALONE of the forty-six scientists who worked on Project Pow, Pete and I had stayed behind. We were fuel experts, minor characters in the drama of the long ditch, and everyone else had a doctor's degree tacked on his name and was a VIP to the back teeth. So they'd all been called to Washington to make a special report to Congress, while Pete and I relaxed and twiddled our thumbs for ten days. This was the third day, this morning when the phone and radio went dead.

"Try the lights," I suggested after a while.

They worked all right. "Television?" said Pete, and turned it on and fussed with the knobs, and got nothing whatever.

We had a beer and stared at each other, scowling, and then went out to see if any of the work gang or the domestic help could help us. There wasn't a soul around.

"Oh damn, they're in Vegas," said Pete. "I forgot, they took the weekend off."

"Let's check on the generators."

Which we did, and of course they were fine, since we did have electricity in all the buildings and only the communications systems were out of whack. So we got in a jeep and drove to the flat furrow, where a company of infantry was quartered, guarding the equipment. They were all there, and I was almighty glad to see them, because things were feeling eerier by the minute.

The captain in charge, Granville, became very unhappy when he heard what was wrong. He was of the infinite-suspicion school. "Damn saboteurs," he said, not explaining why he thought anyone would sabotage our TV. "Corporal, check all the walkie-talkies." The corporal did and they worked handily. "Ought to have a 24-hour guard on that place up there," said the captain, gesturing bitterly toward our living quarters. "All them brains and nobody can light a match on his pants without help. Come on, I'll fix your damn TV."

We three returned to the technicians' quonset and Granville turned on the TV and got a low hum. "Did you think to use this knob?" he asked witheringly. Nothing happened. No picture, just the buzz. He looked slightly less cocky. He fiddled and swore. "Hell," he said, "let's call a serviceman in Vegas."

"You forget the phone's dead too," said Pete mildly.

Granville barked into the mute instrument for three or four minutes, tried to vivify the radio, and began to look a little unsure of himself. "This is nuts," he said. "I've got to go check the radar. No telling what's…" He walked out, mumbling. We trailed after him.

The quonsets and the other buildings were erected on a small hill, perhaps a hundred feet higher than the desert flat. About half a mile from the foot of the hill was the north end of the 20-mile ditch. Ringing the entire proving grounds, which was about 24 by 16 miles in perimeter, were much higher hills, and in them, invisible from here, were gun emplacements and ack-ack batteries and a regiment of men under a colonel who knew more about defending a critical area than anyone else in the U. S. A. Project Pow was well and thoroughly protected. But our telephones weren't working, and we didn't know why.

We piled into the jeep and went down to Captain Granville's quarters. He ordered the radar on—an emergency measure, usually it sat there dead and grotesque-looking, for there was a lot of radar equipment up in the hills, going all the time—and we waited.

ONE of the operators came over to us in five minutes. He was rather green. He stuttered and Granville bleated at him and he got hold of himself and said, "Radar shows a w—wall all around us."

"A what?"

"A wall. It goes up from the foot of the h—hills and we can't find the t—top. It's all around us except for over there," said the corporal, pointing to a pass in the range northwest of us. "There's a break in it there. Don't ask me why."

"A wall," said Captain Granville without emotion. "Sure. Okay, dogface, let's take a look." The corporal changed from green to pink. He escorted the three of us to his screen, moodily biting his lip. Granville watched the screen. After a minute he went to another one. Pete Ashton and I stared at each other, wondering. Finally the captain said, "What did you guys do here a week ago, anyway?" His eyes were a little crossed with anxiety.

"We surpassed the speed of light."

"Well, you also fouled up our radar. This soldier's right, it shows a wall all around the proving grounds." We all stared at the perimeter of the flatland and there was obviously nothing above the hills except fresh air and cloudless sky.

"When did you use the radar last?" I asked the corporal.

"We always test it at seven a.m. sir."

"It was all right this morning?"

"Yes sir."

"Then it wasn't us that did it," Pete said to Granville.

The Captain said a fairly obscene word or two, and looked at the northwest valley where the radar showed no "wall." He said, "Hey!" loudly. We all looked.

It was about three miles off. It looked like a small dark clot of ants. Granville snatched for binoculars and scanned it and without speaking handed the glass to me. The dark clot was a number of horsemen, approaching leisurely along the floor of the pass. There seemed to be a good many of them, and some of them had what looked like plumes in their strangely shaped hats.

Granville began to scream orders. He didn't pause for any analysis of the problem for our benefit, so I'll never know what he thought was approaching; bluster and all, he was a good soldier, and his job was to defend our equipment and persons from anything that threatened. In spite of cockeyed radar and plumed headgear and silent guns in the hills, he knew that something that could be classified as an *enemy* was coming, and he went out to meet it, with nearly every man of his company. They went in jeeps, leaving behind only the radar operators, some eight or ten at most. Everyone had a rifle, and the last jeep roared off within two minutes of Granville's first bellow. He was in the forefront.

I watched through the field glass, describing what happened to Pete Ashton.

The dark mass of horsemen spread out and I saw that they were only the van of a great column of riders. They continued to jog forward toward the nearing jeeps.

The corporal on the radar screen nearest me said, "That wall is all around us now. The gap's closed." It was gibberish insofar as I could see. There wasn't any wall.

The jeeps stopped. The horses stopped. After a moment Granville's jeep began to crawl forward and the horsemen wheeled and rode away; all the jeeps started again and the horses picked up speed. There was a distance of about thirty yards between nags and machines. The jeeps barreled along and I expected to see them run between the horses, but oddly they did not diminish the gap. Not a foot, not an inch, if I could judge from three miles off.

The corporal said conversationally, "The wall's gone at the pass again."

I saw Granville waving his bands for more speed and the jeeps tore over the sand and by heavens, I thought, now they'll be among 'em, now we'll see what happens; but nothing happened except that the horses stayed in front by the same thirty yards. I could fairly hear Granville curse at his driver.

They entered the valley, all of them, vast pack of riders and jeeps alike. I handed the glass quickly to Pete, having hogged it long enough. He told me what happened.

"You're right, they aren't catching up, and they must be doing—I won't even guess what they're doing. Sixty? No horse can do it. Not over sand for minutes and minutes... Now they're curving left. Must be close to a thousand in that mob. Why doesn't Granville shoot at them?"

"They haven't done anything but approach the field."

"That's reason enough to shoot and query later. Now the first horses are out of sight. Lord, I wish I was up there! I wish I could see this close up... There goes the last horse out of sight behind the hill. There go the jeeps." In a minute he lowered the binoculars and handed them to me. "If we're right, and these gentry were called over a Time bridge by our pottering with velocities, Sam," he said slowly, "why are they all mounted on horses that outrun the best jeeps in America? And how come they're all highwaymen? Wouldn't some plain honest citizens trickle through? What did we tap with the calefite and sclerium, Newgate Gaol?"

"Don't ask me, Bradbury."

"I'm just rhetoricalizing, Van Vogt. Don't expect answers. Why hasn't some poor gin-peddler ambled into Reno? Why aren't there weavers, tinkers, beaux, oval-windowed coaches, comb-makers, gypsies leading dancing bears, fops, beggars shamming disease, and ladies in silks and powders, all plumped down into Flagstaff and Cotton-wood and Albuquerque? Why only scamps on the road, highway levelers, the gentlemen of the saber and horse pistols?"

I refused to think. I put up the binoculars again in time to see the first horses reappear in the gut of the pass. They were heading straight for me and I couldn't judge speed worth a whoop. On they came, like a fantastic charge of an unimaginable light brigade. But they weren't stormed at with shot and shell; they were quite unmolested.

I caught glimpses of jeeps behind them. Granville's bunch, still chasing like Keystone Cops after crazily costumed extras. The horsemen came out onto the open plain and canted off right and I could see that the jeeps were now a good sixty or seventy yards behind. The horses drew up and several detached from the main body and trotted out to stand waiting, Granville stood up in the front jeep, for all the world like a cavalryman standing in his stirrups.

One of the riders raised his arm and I saw that he held a pistol in it. There was a small puff of black smoke. Granville swayed and pitched sideways out of the jeep, I would have bet ten dollars on the sick-making certainty that he was dead before he hit the sand.

The radarman said quietly, "That wall's there again, not a blank-blank break in it anywhere. We got a topless wall around us, Mister Scientist, sir."

The jeep in which Granville had been riding stopped cold. Its nose looked as if it were telescoping into itself for no reason. The two men in it rose up as its rear lifted, flung toward me, and dropped onto the shattered hood. The same thing happened to a second vehicle. The others braked to teeth-jolting stops.

Soldiers piled out and their rifles were in their hands. Some of them flung themselves prone and others stood in rifle-range standing position. They looked as though they were firing into the brown of the highwaymen jerking with the recoil of their rifles.

There was only one catch to this idea. No rider fell, no horse kicked and screamed at the impact of a jacketed slug.

Oh, yes. There wasn't any noise either. They were rather less than three miles away, but I couldn't hear a single rifle-crack.

The soldiers continued to go through their mad, silent motions. The thousand horsemen turned and trotted easily across the desert toward our big ditch.

I handed the binoculars to Pete.

"Wall's still there," said the corporal. "What do you make of it, anyway?"

I couldn't tell him, I couldn't even think. I had the suspicion that I had suddenly gone stark, staring insane.

Pete fulfilled his promise of the early morning, and was sick as a dog all over the sand of Project Pow.

CHAPTER FOUR

WE waited in an unformed row for them. We had decided against a violent reception. After all, there were only eleven of us and such a mob of them...

There were eight radar operators and a cook who hadn't gone into Vegas with the rest because of a headache. There was Pete Ashton, and there was me. Quite an army.

The horsemen drew up a little distance off, and two of them moved out toward us. One was tall, as tall as me, with a fair face and a black wig; his clothing was beautiful, velvet and satin, and I had the feeling I'd seen him before. Then I remembered the newspaper description of the first highwayman, the one who had bushrangered the Blackbird bus. I saw the opal stickpin in the Flemish lace, and knew it was him. The other was fat and small and looked moldy. As though he'd been dug up from potter's field after a bad job of hanging.

The soldiers who'd gone out with Granville were still over at the mouth of the pass. We'd stopped looking at them, because they didn't seem to be doing anything but run back and forth and make indecipherable motions with their hands. The only reasonable theory was that they'd all lost their minds.

The tall horseman removed his black, silver-laced cocked hat and swept it around in a kind of mocking bow and said, "Your servant, gentles all. I have the honor to be Galloping Jonas, king of the royal scamps, and this is my companion in roguery, Gothic Beall." The moldy one smirked. Two more horses moved up beside them, carrying another pair of characters. "This is Prime Minister William O'Shay, and yonder is Prime Minister Robert Mac Lorn. I must acquaint you further, gentles, that this horse I sit is none other than the famed Tess, who galloped from Lunnon to John o' Groat's in a single night." He paused as if for murmurs of applause.

Nobody said anything for a minute, and then Pete husked and said, "*Two* prime ministers?"

"Assuredly," said Galloping Jonas. "Behind me ride seventeen in all, worthies and gallant scoundrels to a man. Greater thieves than any of us poor honest purse-pur-loiners, eh?" The whole crowd of them, easily a thousand, set up a kind of hollow, cackling laughter. I took it that Jonas was boss, and if he made a joke, you laughed.

His accent was something frightful. I'd known many Englishmen, but nothing to equal the guttural, mumbling speech that came from Jonas's handsome mouth had I ever heard. I recalled the professor who'd labeled it authentic Norfolk, vintage 1725. You couldn't have proved it by me, but I knew I had to strain and think and guess like the devil to understand his sentences. I can't reproduce them in print, not with ease anyway. ("Servants," for instance, he pronounced something like "saarnt.")

"Now," he said, sitting back in the saddle, "we've come a deal of distance and we're tired. What inns may there be hereabouts, eh?" He waved a hand languidly at me. "I speak to you, fellow," he said, "knave, scullion, or what ha' ye, you in the ill-begot costume there, I asked you, where might we bed down?"

PALE eyes were fastened on my face and I knew this wasn't the time to ask him questions or to procrastinate unnecessarily. I gestured up the hill toward our Quonsets and personnel buildings. "There's shelter," I said, "but not enough beds for so many."

"If it has floors we can sleep in it," said Gothic Beall, the dead-looking one.

"Aye," said Jonas. He turned his horse's head north, and the whole cavalcade got into motion. "Be where I can find ye when I'm rested," he called to us, and passed and disappeared as the concourse filed in behind him. I scanned it as it passed, and for the first time saw that there were women among the riders, several score at least.

"Who are they?" said Pete beside me, and I said, "Doxies, what else?" before I'd even actually remembered that I knew the archaic word. "I don't mean the dames," said Pete. "I mean the whole impossible lot of 'em, seventeen prime ministers and all."

"I'll tell you who they are," said the corporal whose name was Kemp. "They're spooks."

"That does seem reasonable," I said.

"I'm not kidding, buster," said Kemp angrily. "I don't suppose you noticed the horses?"

"Terrific chunks of horseflesh," said Pete, staring after the mob.

"Sure, sure." Kemp spat onto the sand. I admired him for that, because my own mouth was dry as snakeskin. "Great big powerful chargers, aren't they? There's only one thing wrong with them." We both looked at him and the cook, Lester, said "What?" and Kemp after a moment told us. I didn't doubt him, because he was anything but an hysterical type, and since his first discovery of the invisible "wall" on radar he hadn't turned a hair.

I devoutly hoped that this would be the last little surprise the day would offer us. After dead telephones, blind TV, crazy radar, the unseeable wall, noiseless shots from Army rifles, a thousand ancient horsemen and 17 prime ministers, horses that outdistanced jeeps, Galloping Jonas and his accent and his horse pistols, well, I was about ready to knock off. So I hoped that Kemp's revelation would prove to be the finale.

It wasn't, of course; a lot of good men were going to die, and my world was going to rock off its foundations before the sun set. I didn't know this, though. So I hoped.

What Kemp had said was, "Those horses, chums, ain't alive. I mean they're *dead*. Because why? Because I was watching the big joker's nag all the time he was talking. I was raised in Kentucky and I know horses." He took a deep breath. "That horse, and all the rest of 'em, stamped and shifted and trotted away just as bright as you please, right? Looked just great. Only trouble was, *not a damn one of them was breathing*. Their chests were as still as a rock in the sun. Their sides didn't heave, even after that gallop out there." He looked from Pete to Lester to me. "Them ponies," he said firmly, "are as dead as roast beef sandwiches. There isn't a breath or a heartbeat in the whole stinking stable."

CHAPTER FIVE

"LET'S get over to those soldiers," said Pete shakily.

"Not me," said Kemp. There's something just as wrong over there as there is up here." He waved a hand at the personnel buildings, where a thousand or so horses stood quietly, without a single guard to watch them, without a grain of feed or a single hobble or tied-up rein to keep them from wandering off. Every man and woman of the fantastic horde had vanished into the huts, where they were presumably sleeping, lined up on the hard floors like so many bums in a cheap flophouse. "Look at that," went on Kemp. "They just stand there. You don't have to halter a dead horse. Not a saddle taken off, either. Dead... And I ain't going up to the pass, either, because there's something so damn wrong with the boys I don't even want to come close to it."

"What are you going to do?" I asked him.

"Find every rifle and every cartridge I can, and see about settin' up a fort around here somewhere, I got a notion when the play-actors are done sackin', they'll be looking for us. I'm gonna be ready for them," He stared at us defiantly. "Ten guys with rifles ought to be able to take a thousand with them cap pistols. Even when three of us are civilians."

We left him to search for weapons, and Pete and I, with two soldiers and the cook Lester, took two jeeps and rattled off toward the pass where the company was still milling about on the sand.

When we'd come within a hundred yards, they'd spotted us and were waiting, some standing alone, others bunched beside the two wrecked jeeps. What in hell had smashed up those hoods so thoroughly? There were three bodies laid out, Granville and two GI's.

"Looks as if they went full tilt into a stone wall," said Pete. Then he snapped, "Stop!" and automatically I braked to a fast halt. "They did," Pete glanced at me and back to the soldiers. "They did run into a wall. The wall that showed on Kemp's radar. We saw them do it."

He was right and yet, how could you believe it or even think about it? There was nothing out here but desert and a couple of Joshua trees and a little creosote bush and a lot of dry, hot air. I gazed at the crumpled metal of the jeeps and at the soldiers who were grouped so oddly, staring at us silently, and I knew Pete was right but I couldn't believe it. I stood up. "Hey!" I shouted to the infantrymen, who were about, 200 feet away, "What happened?"

A dozen mouths flew open; scores of arms gestured wildly. Not a sound came to us through the bright silent air.

I moved as if I were slogging through a dream, incredulous and skeptical of everything that existed in this insane day. I came within a yard of a private who was yelling at me, quite soundless though I could see his throat muscles strain and bulge. I halted, and inch by inch went forward, feet dragging, heart crashing like rhythmic thunder in an aching chest, with my hands before me as if I were blind. And there it was, the wall.

MY hands gradually pressed tight against it, though all my sinews flinched from contact. It was solid and without roughness or flaw, smooth and neither cold nor hot; it went straight up higher than I could reach, it had no end-ing in the sand but went down, possibly for miles, for I dredged up a heap of sand at its foot with one shoe, and could not discover the bottom of this sight-undiscernible, occulty-reared, quiet impossible wall.

"It must be a mile high," said Pete beside me, and I leaped and said "Aagh!" because I'd been lost in horror. "That's why we can't hear them shouting. What the hell did this, Sam?" He pounded my shoulder with a fist, his face pale and tight with nerves, verging on hysteria. "Did we do it? We did…didn't we, Sam? With our bloody toys and—"

I slapped him in the face. I meant only to shock him into calm, but strung up like a banjo string myself, I put a lot more force into the blow than I'd intended. It knocked him down.

He came up from the sand at me like a turpentined wolverine. His eyes were bulging and without intelligence. I clipped him on the jaw and he had my neck in his hands. We fell together, while Lester and the two radarmen screamed at us. Pete Ashton and I were embroiled in the first fight we'd ever had.

I outweighed him, had inches of reach on him, but he was as wiry and rugged as they come. It was anybody's brawl. I took a short hard left in the gut that bent me down and then his fists were bashing me in the face, right and left and right without pause, and I curled over prawn-wise to protect my head while lights popped and blazed in my skull and pain shot through me in jolts of ragged fire. I shoved one arm out straight and fast and by good luck connected with his ribs, which pushed him back long enough to let me get a gasp of wind and clear my eyes of hair and blood.

I went after him then. I boxed in college, was on the fencing team and cross-country too. My 'dozing of the big trench had hardened me to top form. It was like pitting a heavyweight champion against a bantamweight. In two minutes I'd stretched him out flat on his back.

He raised his face and stared at me. We heaved for air, glaring madly, and then slowly the anger and ferocity went out of both of us. I put out a hand and he took it and I set him on his feet.

"Damned if you aren't a fighting cock when you're aroused, boy," I said. I gave him a handkerchief for his nosebleed. We began to laugh.

There was no more sense in the laughter than there'd been in the fight; but the two of them saved our reason, I'm sure. Till that quick raging tangle we'd been getting stiffer with fear, more appalled at the unknown and the unbelievable, till we were both ready to crack wide open. The violence purged us, the laughing knitted us back together again.

From that moment on, the wild adventure might scare us, it might maim and destroy us, but it could not drive us into insanity or cowardice. We'd eased the tension in the oldest way—the good animal way, by scrapping—forgetting to think and just mixing it up. From there on, we quit racking our brains needlessly for explanations of each new idiocy of the universe; we took what came and fought it as we would have fought, say, a normal attack by an enemy in war.

I thank God for Pete Ashton, as I know he did for me.

Lester and the others were standing around us, not precisely grinning, but looking as if they might at any second. After the first amazement, they'd enjoyed our tussle. I think they felt some relief themselves. "Sam," said the cook, "what is this wall, anyway?" Which brought us back to our problems, but with clearer (if pretty well bashed up) heads.

"I think it's some kind of force field," I said, with dim memories of such things in long-ago reading. "It's beyond anything our government can have set up, and I'd say that went for any other country's science, too. I don't know what put it here. It's possible that some reaction to our busting the light barrier caused it. If it did, I can't explain it any more than you can."

Pete, mopping up gore absently, asked the radar operators, "You couldn't find the top of it, could you?"

"No sir."

"Might it be that there's a roof too? That we're really caged into a walloping big room, 24 miles by 16?"

"Could be, sir. We didn't try 'em straight up."

"We'll have to do that. Out of sheer curiosity." He gave me the handkerchief, which I took one look at and dropped into a creosote bush. We both put our palms flat against the unseen wall.

On the other side, the company of soldiers, who had crowded close to watch the fight, shifted backward a little; and one man, a short red-headed fellow, put his hands against the wall opposite my own. There was no pressure communicated through the barrier, but so far as I could see, our hands were actually touching one another. Pete got his head as close as possible to them and said, "Looks as though the thing isn't any thicker than a sheet of paper. By the way, Sam, you get any sensation?"

"I hadn't noticed it." Then it did seem to me that a tingling, a very minor charge as of slight electrical leakage, was noticeable. I told him, "Yeah. . .it's a force field of some kind, Sam, there's no doubt."

He shook his head. "How it ties in with Galloping Jonas and seventeen prime ministers, I refuse to guess."

We left the infantry, mute and impotent to help us beyond their great transparent mystery and slowly rolled back to the proving grounds.

The horses still stood patiently on the hill. No highwaymen were in evidence yet. We looked for Kemp, but couldn't see him. There was a row of tents near the launching platform, in which the soldiers had lived until today. I started at one end and Pete at the other, peering into each one, looking for the absent Kemp and his four colleagues. In the third tent I inspected, there was a girl. She was asleep, she was lovely, and of all the impossible things that had occurred this day, she was the most unlikely!

CHAPTER SIX

SHE wore a gown of green velvet, silver cloth shoes and embroidered stockings; a diamond-headed bodkin was thrust casually through the front curls of her blonde hair. Her skin was creamy, the lashes of her closed eyes very long and heavy. Her low-cut bodice was beautifully filled, and her waist was as slim as Scarlet O'Hara's. She looked strangely normal to me, as she lay there on the army cot with her red lips a little parted... Of course she seemed normal! She resembled at least forty jackets off the historical novels in our library. You could see her counterpart being wooed by Rock Brandon on a thousand movie screens across the country tonight. She was Nell Gwyn, or possibly Amber ...

She was too good. "Mirage," I muttered huskily, and reached out to touch her on the cheek, with perfectly decent motives of reassuring myself of her substantiality; and found my wrist caught in a biting grip, and the point of the long deadly bodkin pressed gently to my palm. "Whoa!" I yelped. "I only wanted—"

"What every man wants," she said, using a quite unprintable word instead of *man* however. Her opened eyes were dark blue and coldly angry. "I ought to run you through the hand for a lesson." Then she let me go and leaned back, sighing; but kept the rapier-like hairpin ready. "I expected Jonas," she said. "Not one o' you culls. What lock d'ye cut, anyway?"

"Beg your pardon?" I said, sitting down on a campstool.

"What d'ye do?" she said impatiently. "What lay are you on? How do you earn your living, for the love of heaven?"

"I'm a fuel expert."

"What, you sell wood?"

"No, not quite that. I—" and I stopped. What could I tell the wench in her own language that would explain calefite to her? Probably nothing. I tried. "I work on oils and vapors and gasses, which we put into ships to make them travel quickly. Not on the water, but through the air, and perhaps through the far sky to other worlds."

There was one instant when I believed I saw a dozen emotions chase themselves through her lovely great eyes: astonishment, comprehension, unbelief and horror, but overpowering all of them, an intelligent knowledge of what I meant. The next moment she was jeering, "When did you crawl out of Bedlam, honey?" and her eyes were flat and unreadable, and I thought I had mistaken the things I'd seen.

We spoke, she in the cant and jargon of 18th-Century London, I in as basic an English as I could manage; and I tried to tell her what I did here, what Project Pow was all about, even something about the light barrier. It was suddenly necessary that I tell this full-blown girl about myself. And such a need I hadn't felt since early college days.

Then, when I asked her where she came from and what date it was, she was silent; and the guttural growl of Galloping Jonas came over my shoulder. "I've been scouring for ye, Barbary," said he. I jumped up, turning, and the muzzle of a pistol waved me aside. "What are you telling my doxy, hick?"

TAKING it that hick signified the same thing to him as it did to me, I was going to smack him; but Barbary, the girl, was quicker than I. She was off the cot and clawing for his eyes and he had to holster the gun and use both hands to fend her off. "Neither your doxy, nor anyone else's!" she was yelling. Jonas backed, grinning, and her fingers caught at the long full foppish black wig and tore it down off the front of his head, bringing the cocked hat with it, so that he was blinded for a few seconds.

Now if this had happened an hour before, I suppose I wouldn't have done a thing. I'd been awed to the point of inaction by all the insanity of the day. But Pete and I had shucked off our awe and wanted to do something; besides which, I liked this girl Barbary. And I didn't care two cents for Mister Galloping Jonas and his good, dead nag, Tess.

One step took me to his side, and while he swore, muffled in the great periwig, I snatched both the horse pistols from his belt and reversed them so that when he emerged, gasping and red in the face, from the fallen mass of curls, he found himself covered by his own guns. They were flintlocks, and I had only a hazy idea of how to fire them. But I was ready to try.

"Curse blight ye," said Jonas very quietly, and the ridiculous phrase came out as a dire threat from his hard lips. He was shaved as bald as a cue ball, and the loss of the black wig turned him into a far more evil figure than I could have imagined. He moved slowly toward me. I cocked the pistols.

There was a painful sharp prick in my right ear. "Hand 'em back to him," said Barbary, "or you'll get six inches of pin through your brains, cully." Meekly I held out the pistols to Jonas. I felt certain that the wench was not joking. The pain withdrew from my ear as Jonas tore the weapons out of my hands.

"And you, Jonas," said she, "may I suggest you don't spatter his guts on the wall till we're surer of where we are, eh?"

Jonas gave a brief growl and holstered the guns and picked up his wig and hat, brushed them off tidily and adjusted them to his bare skull. "Aye. When I've done with him, though, he'll crave a lead pill in the noggin as he craves salvation! Now come out o' here, we've work to do." He dived out onto the sand, and the treacherous, ungrateful Barbary followed him swiftly. I went after them. I was much angrier at the outlandish, out-of-Time wench than I really had any reason or right to be.

CHAPTER SEVEN

THERE were about forty highwaymen standing among the tents. I looked for Pete Ashton, saw him with Lester and a couple of soldiers, and walked over to them.

"What's the matter, Sam, did Jonas catch you with his girl?" asked Pete.

"All very innocent," I said, "and she wound up pushing a knife in my ear." I squinted around through the dry, steaming air. "Where's Kemp got to?" He and six other radarmen were missing.

"I dunno," said Pete, "but I'll bet he's fixing himself a fort somewhere, and I wish we were with him. It looks like all hell is ready to bust loose."

The visitors were scowling and talking excitedly, and even though a lot of them were within earshot, I couldn't understand their growling speech; they had to go almighty slow to be intelligible to me. I saw Galloping Jonas speaking earnestly with Barbary, while the moldy-looking Gothic Beall listened with his fat face bunched up worriedly. Figuring I could comprehend Barbary better than the others, I strolled toward them, trying to look innocuous.

Well, I caught two or three sentences, the words "oils, gas, other worlds"—then Jonas broke in, "Have you your lexicon?" and Barbary dug into her skirts and handed him a small scarlet-covered book. He thumbed it, muttering. Then he said, quite clearly, "Ah, 'tis zaminfler and fufre, as I recollected!" I had only time to wonder what outlandish items might fufre and zaminfler be, when the repellent

Beall turned his head and saw me. "Come here," he said, crooking a dirty finger. I stepped over to them. Pete was behind me, and I heard him murmur, "Ten bucks says you can't steal that book," before Jonas' hateful voice thundered an astonishing question at me.

"On what world were ye born?"

"This one," I said automatically; then thinking I had misunderstood him, or his meaning, "America."

Jonas squinted at me as if he wouldn't have believed me on the well-known stack of Good Books. "Are ye trying to tell me you were born *here*? Then your ancestors—"

"Here, and some generations back, England."

"This isn't England?" he said, eyes popping. Barbary clapped a hand over her lush mouth, and Gothic Beall turned a putty shade.

"Certainly not. It's America, and the year's 1963."

"Yes, it would be," he muttered, and the astonishing implications of that statement had time only to begin sinking into my brain when he went on: "Are things so different in America, then, from England? I refer not to the landscape, which is unholy enough to bristle your back teeth, but..." he gestured at my clothes the radar installations, the launching platform in the distance, "...whence all this? Answer me, ye jumbling maunder?"

"Whence your seventeen prime ministers?" I rapped back at him, "Whence horses that don't breathe?"

And at that instant, before he could either reply or haul out his horse pistols to blast me, as he looked mad enough to do, there came the loveliest sound in the world. It was the flat hard crack of a rifle.

A highwayman who was standing a dozen feet off swayed, opened his mouth to speak, and pitched on his face in a flurry of satin and ostrich feathers.

JONAS roared, "Get t'others!" and made one magnificent leap and landed in the saddle of his good nag Tess, who had been standing beside him, placidly shifting from hoof to hoof and not breathing. Beall and the rest ran for their horses, leaving Pete and me and Lester and the GI's. Also leaving Barbary, who'd evidently mislaid her mount. She looked swiftly around her as the place erupted, another shot came and a second gentleman of the road hit the sand; horses were plunging and leaping over the tent ropes, one charged full tilt into a tent and brought it down, recovered balance and galloped on, and still Barbary could not locate an empty saddle. Then she screamed, because I had grabbed her firmly and energetically by the waist.

"What a time for passion," said Pete, looking around to see if he could spot the rifleman. "Hot-blooded ol' Sam!"

"Funny man," I barked, "where'd those slugs come from?"

"The ditch," said Lester, the cook. "Look at there, they've got a barricade in the big ditch!"

"Come on," I said, and hoisted Barbary off her feet, tucked her squirming body under my arm, and ran.

Now the great trench was, as I've said, twenty miles long and 60 yards wide. Here at the end of it, it was sunk into the earth a depth of about four feet (3.875, to be exact—how well I remember those blueprints). Running at our best speed, the little knot of us pounded into it down a runway at the side of the launching platform; and 200 yards away were the trucks.

It was just here that I believed someone had shot me in the tail. Talk about fiery, lancing pains... I dropped Barbary on the concrete and swore, touching myself tenderly to see if I was actually half shot away; and the wench rolled over and grinned up at me, waving that damned diamond-headed bodkin cheerfully. "Think yourself lucky I didn't put it through your spine," she jeered. Then I'd kicked it out of her hand, urgently, and wrestled her up and was dragging her, kicking and trying to bite, toward the trucks.

Once I looked over my shoulder. Jonas and his crew were just pouring down the hillside from the quonsets, all thousand or so of them. Knowing how those could go, I wasn't sure I could cover the remaining hundred yards before they flashed over that half-mile between me and them. If I dropped Barbary—but I wouldn't, I wanted her; as hostage, maybe, as the carrier of a small scarlet book, certainly, and even with my rump smarting from her wicked stab, I wanted her because she was herself, a glorious, wild, impossible dame.

Love? That fast? That's for storybooks. But attraction—oh, man, yes!

So, I kept tight hold on her, and I ran, staggering with the pain, panting, down the hard floor of the big ditch.

THE others had reached the trucks and were climbing in. Pete glanced back, saw me in difficulties. At once he was hammering back toward me, yelling.

"Drop her, you dope! You'll never make it!" He didn't know I was wounded, thought I was simply tired and burdened with Barbary. "Help me with her," I gasped as he reached us, "She's important." He took my word for it and snatched her left arm. I had her right arm and then we were hauling her between us, her toes dragging and banging a tattoo on the concrete.

Jonas at the head of his fast-recruited mob was halfway to the launching platform.

The trucks seemed to be a hell of a distance off.

Horses going at 70 mph. The world—or maybe I—had really gone off its rocker.

We were almost there. The near truck loomed up sidelong, just ahead now, and I tried to speed up and fell over my feet, dragging Barbary (screeching malignancies) down on top of me. Pete let her go, still not convinced that she ought to be held; he started to help me up and Barbary shot away on all fours like a great fancy animal escaping an open trap. I twisted and coiled to go after her; Pete's well-meaning fumbling at me held me back for a moment. Then I was sprinting like a miler, aching wound clean forgotten. We did perhaps forty yards and then I launched out and tackled her around the thighs. We hit the iron-hard floor of the trench as though we'd been propelled out of a circus cannon.

Barbary looked at me and touched her raw-scraped cheek, and I'm blasted if she didn't grin, "You're a rare cully," she said. I took it as tribute, smiled back at her, then gripped her very hard by that perfect twenty-inch waist and yanked her to her feet.

One fast look told me that Jonas' boys were nearly to the ditch.

Bellowing at Pete to get on to the trucks, I began staggering back with the girl, who was once more wriggling snakily and swatting at me with raking fingernails.

I sort of doubted that I'd make it this time.

CHAPTER EIGHT

PETE was in the truck, leaning over the side with his arms out toward me. His face was all one sick worried expression. I could hear the no-longer-muted thunder of the dead horseflesh coming up behind, not in the ditch, for concrete would have made a very different sound, but along the sides. Should I chuck the girl down? Hell, after this long... I gathered myself and made a sort of flying pounce at the truck. Hurling Barbary up to Pete, who took her under the arms and jerked her over the side. I clambered up myself just as the first shot whanged out at me from the pistols of that pale-eyed anachronism, Galloping Jonas.

He missed—not by much, I think. I heard steel ring at the impact of the slug, and then I was topping the side, falling on my shoulder inside. Instantly I had whirled and was taking a rifle from the hands of Corporal Kemp. His tough face smirked briefly into mine.

"I seen skirt-crazy guys in my time, mister, but you're the limit. The real brass-plated limit."

Then we were firing into the press.

They came streaming along both sides of the big furrow, their horses slowed now to almost normal horse speed; and like Indians around a circle of wagons, they fired in, whooping, as they passed and turned to arc back and come at us again. Jonas had gone, was out of sight somewhere on the desert behind his lines of weird henchmen.

Kemp had done a beautiful job of arranging the trucks. They were of several types: small vans used for carrying material and pickups with varying side heights, low to fairly high. He'd driven them, he and his men, down here into the ditch, parking them in a rough circle, six trucks with a seventh right in center to which it might be necessary to retreat if things got hot. Kemp must have seen a lot of old Western movies…and it *was* a good arrangement.

Kemp, Pete, Ashton, Barbary and I were in a pickup whose sides were about two feet high. The eight others were scattered among three more pickups, with the two vans broadside to the ramparts of the trench. Our three rifles poured lead into the advancing horde, while the GIs fired as they passed and retreated.

Barbary—about the time I was letting off my fourth shot—decided that she'd join her compatriots. She hoisted herself to her feet and was about to jump to the ground when I grabbed for her ankles. She dodged back, grinned, and then shrieked. She flopped flat beside me, swearing coarsely.

"What happened, baby?" I asked, thinking she'd been shot.

"Some obscenitied vulgar word put a blanked pill through my strammel," she said, her face pale and eyes raging. "Near sliced my nab, the so-and-so!" Digging the strange cant words from the oaths, I deduced that a bullet had gone through her hair—close to the scalp. "Keep yourself down, then," I told her, "Or your pals will be burying you tomorrow."

"They'll carve your guts long afore then," she said.

A charming child. Sighing, I turned my back on her and took up the sharp shooting again.

NOW I had done more than a little shooting in my time. Ducks on the farm, crows at extreme range, deer and rabbit in college days—my eye is pretty average good. I found that to knock a man off a horse when he's coming obliquely at you at forty yards is not too difficult a trick. Pete said afterwards that he hadn't hit one in three; Kemp had a rifleman's medal and probably did as well as I, so in the first dozen minutes of the highwaymen's wild charge I suppose we must have killed and wounded a total of 150 between us. Had they been charging directly at us, we'd have been mincemeat within seconds; as it was they were practically sitting ducks.

They banged away at us with a will, but did no damage at all. This was no reflection on their marksmanship, of course; just try hitting a small target forty yards off, using a flintlock pistol charged with old-style black powder, while sticking to a galloping horse.

Then they drew off to the desert, and—presuming they were out of range—held a council.

"Look," said Kemp, lifting himself to his knees and gesturing, "What about them?" He was pointing at the dead, an unholy lot of them, still and stiffening in their finery.

"What about 'em?" asked Pete.

"No horses. Not one bloody horse lying cold, or even screaming with a wound. I told you, they're all dead."

I happened to look at Barbary as he said it, and saw her grimace at him evilly.

What in hell *was* the answer?

Kemp shouted, "You guys okay back there?"

The soldiers answered. Two were shot, one dying. "Not so bad," said Kemp without emotion. "Score the first round to Uncle Sam's pride." He must have seen something disapproving in my face. "What's the matter, doc," he said sourly, "d'you still think you're fighting human beings? You figure them bodies are *people?*" He laughed briefly and took a bead on the distant enemy. He shot—and one fell. "Come on, shoot," he said. "The only way we'll finish this fight on our feet is if we knock over every damn one of 'em." Feeling that he was right, and deliberately conquering my prejudice against shooting fish in a barrel, I began to fire slowly and carefully.

My bodkin-stab gave a twinge. It reminded me of Barbary. I glanced over at the wench, and saw her lowering herself silently over the side. I caught a wrist in time, pulled her up and shook her ferociously. "I'll have to tie you up," I said.

"Oh, don't do that," she said, alarmed. "I'll be good, I'll stay." She looked anxiously at me. "Word o' honor," she said.

What the devil did it matter, anyway? "All right," I said. "But give me that red book now."

She backed away across the truck, shaking her head. In no mood to fool around, I went after her, snatched her arms, held both with one hand and searched through the green velvet gown with the other. She bit and wriggled, as usual. She was a powerful woman and an angry (or frightened?) one, but finally I held the small volume in my palm. Then I let her go, and she sank to her knees, shivering with fear or suppressed rage.

I knelt beside Pete Ashton and before I started firing again I said, "There was a matter of a bet." I handed him the book. "You owe me ten bucks," I said.

CHAPTER NINE

THEY came again, but this time they had learned caution.

As they deployed, many of them on foot, I put one slug into a horse. I took keen aim and could almost hear the lead *thunk* into its chest. And absolutely nothing happened.

Spread in a long line to our left, about a hundred highwaymen ran at us, bent over into small targets. When they had nearly reached the side of the trench, a mob of horsemen, who had recrossed farther down, came galloping and yelling at us from the right.

Letting Pete take the foe on foot, Kemp and I concentrated on the riders. I sprawled a big ugly devil over his horse's tail and knocked a slim fop sideways to be dragged in his stirrup, saw Gothic Beall and aimed at him but missed; then they were at the lip of the ditch and instead of canting off to go along its edge, they lifted their nags into the air and flew at us in a cresting wave of velvet and satin and steel and broad unbreathing horseflesh.

Now no charger, be he living or as dead as last year's television comic, can jump twenty yards through the air and land on a pickup truck while maintaining his balance and keeping his rider in the saddle. I realized this in the split second when I saw them all rising from the ground; and that tiny bit of hope kept me from panicking. I shot very fast and put two men out of the brawl while the nags were still dropping; then as they touched concrete, with a jarring clangor like insane thunder, I killed a man with a beefy, ruddy face who was just going to fall out of his seat anyway. I was a little sorry I'd done it—it was too much like kicking a fellow who's teetering on a cliff—for as they hit, more than half of the horses fell forward, spilling their masters onto the floor of the big ditch.

"See 'em go!" roared somebody, I think Kemp. "No Kentucky trotter would be that clumsy, by Gosh!"

Perhaps the highwaymen had never leaped their mounts into a depression before that day. I don't know. Certainly they had called on their eerie beasts to perform a fairly simple stunt; but neither men nor animals could have been at all used to it, because even the nags who kept their feet lost their riders.

That was the only thing that saved us in that second attack.

The scamps on foot were racing toward us from the other side, now standing and firing their flintlocks, now dashing forward, heedless of those who dropped beside them. The foremost reached the lip, jumped down and were piled in writhing heaps by the Army rifles of Kemp and his men. I ploughed a bullet into one of them who had been aiming at us from an uncomfortably close distance and switched back to the erstwhile horsemen.

These were in sad case. There were broken bones among them, and a number of them were stunned. I believe the heart was out of them even before we began to take toll at the deadly range.

THEY attacked bravely enough, but now, with the trucks looming over them and heavy rifles crashing without letup, they had small chance. I fired, moved the muzzle slightly, and fired again. Then an automatic weapon began chattering beside me. It was Kemp with a Thompson sub—and that did it. They collapsed like tenpins, like rag dolls, like 18th-Century highwaymen under 20th-Century firepower. My Lord, it was brutal.

When Barbary screamed and buried her face in her skirt, I could hardly blame her, for I wanted to do the same thing.

The sounds of gurgling, dying men sickened me to the soul. I shot a man who was coming up over the side, saw his face go all to strawberry-colored jam, and his hands whiten on the truck and cling desperately for seconds before his carcass fell off. I saw a fellow whom I recognized as Prime Minister William O'Shay, and as he leveled a gigantic pistol at my head from ten feet away, I shot him in the chest, and watched him jolt backward and spin around and collapse on the concrete. Then they started to snatch at bridles, and haul themselves into the saddles, panicky and pale, and I couldn't have killed another if my life hung in the balance.

Kemp, sensibly enough, I suppose, fed them another burst before they had pounded away down the trench to temporary safety.

The men who had been running at us fled now too, appalled by the chattering Thompson.

The nine of us still on our feet at the beginning of that second charge had accounted for an estimated 175 highwaymen.

"What a beastly, bloody butchery," said Pete Ashton, dabbing at his face with a handkerchief, where a bullet had torn his cheek and ear. Kemp called impassively, "How many still with us?" and Lester, the cook, shouted from out of sight somewhere, "Two here." Altogether, four answered, accounting for six. Nine still okay.

A soldier in the truck opposite ours in the circle, who was facing toward the south end of the ditch, cried that a lot of the enemy were getting down the walls into our flat furrow. We all stood up to look. They were descending on foot, letting the horses follow slowly and avoiding the catastrophe of the previous charge. Kemp reconnoitered, said that there seemed to be no subsidiary force forming, and ordered everybody into the south trucks, "And I suggest that you bash this dame on the skull and leave her here," he said pointedly to me. "I don't trust her with all these guns lyin' loose."

I looked at Barbary. "Give me your promise?" I asked. "You won't try to use them on us?"

She looked at me for a long moment before she slowly nodded. "Trust me," she said quietly. Damned if I know why I did...but I did.

As we climbed down into the center of the circle the last thing I saw was her white face, very proud and hating; behind her rose the groans and faint calls of the sorely wounded highwaymen in the ditch.

We got into the truck that faced south. It had high steel sides behind which we could stand upright, only stooping a little, about as safe as legionnaires behind stone parapets—which is to say that only a well-aimed or a chance shot in the head would hit us. There were six of us in this vehicle and three in the one to our right. About five score of the enemy were massed in the trench, just within range of our rifles. Kemp and several others began shooting methodically and swiftly as the weird mounts that did not breathe or feel bullets moved into a canter and then a gallop toward us.

Suddenly there was a crash from immediately in back of us, and Lester, the cook, grunted and slammed forward, struck the steel and slid to the floor, twitching feebly. *Barbary,* I thought, and even as I turned to shoot her, felt my stomach turn over with nausea. I felt a powerful attraction for the lying, murderous wench…and I was going to put a bullet in that lovely breast.

Thank God, it hadn't been Barbary! One of the wounded highwaymen had managed to crawl under the trucks behind us and lever himself up over the side to loose off a horse pistol; as I brought my muzzle around to take him, his mouth fell open and he disappeared. Dead, I suppose, before he hit—his last dying act the tug at the trigger.

Kemp, cursing, sent one of his men into the middle truck to guard our rear. "And if that thing in skirts so much as shows her kisser, blast it," he said between his teeth.

Then we turned and took the charge of the suicide squadron.

CHAPTER TEN

NOW this was the most terrible, the most terrifying attack of the day. They came at us at a speed that I would judge somewhere between fifty and seventy miles an hour. I was far too busy with the gun to think consciously of the fantastic elements of all this, but underneath I'm sure I was icy with fear of horses that could easily outdistance the fastest thing on legs, the cheetah. But as I say, there was no time to exclaim *what can they be* to myself...

As I pumped slug after slug into the riders, I saw that when a horse lost its man, it shot off to one side or the other, and came to a skidding halt by the sides of the ditch, so that the main attack, which was about thirty yards broad at its van, was not snarled by riderless nags. Somewhere there was a tremendous intelligence at work.

The courage of the rogues was magnificent. How does that old poem go... "Stormed at with shot and shell, boldly they rode and well." It might have been written for Jonas' lads.

They came at our trucks with no slacking of the speed, and I felt rather than saw Kemp drop his rifle and pick up the sub-machine gun. In a second it began belching death at them. Still they came, and now the horses were lifting once more in a great leap that took them soaring over us; and at the top of that jump the men launched themselves sidelong out of the saddles and fell among us, so many six-foot projectiles of human flesh, guns holstered and hands reaching out for us.

If a man opened a car door and leaped when the auto was tearing along at 50 per, he wouldn't hit what he was aiming for, nor would he survive the crazy jump. It was just as bad, this wild try of theirs to overwhelm us by dropping atop us from rocketing demons shaped like horses. It was not their main plan, though, it was a kind of furious kamikaze attack, in the wake of which came the true storming of the bastions.

The ranks behind had gradually; slowed until they rode at an almost normal speed; possibly thirty horses flew over us, or struck the sides of the trucks and crumpled down out of sight. Then, as bodies fell among us, some of them knocking our men left and right, the second line came to thundering halt and those horsemen fired at us, standing in stirrups and blazing away with flintlocks in every fist. The inside of the truck was pure hell, a racket of grisly sound as shrieks and groans rose from a thrashing, milling chaos of broken bodies. A dozen or more of the hurtling figures had dropped into our particular fortress from the soaring animals. The couple of them who were not killed or knocked out were grappling with soldiers, and the lead hail ripped in among us with fine impartiality.

KEMP was down, whether dead or dying I did not know. I felt a hot whine go along my cheek, knew I was shot though how badly I couldn't tell, and bending, snatched the Thompson gun from the roof and shoved it over the side. Luckily I knew the principle of the weapon, though I'd never held one before. I let the highwaymen have a burst, muzzle swiveling at the level of their chests, and cut into the second rank as the first crumpled. Rifles began banging again beside me, and I heard Pete Ashton yell and abruptly my weapon was empty.

"Get down here," said Kemp clearly through the melee. I knelt, and he told me how to reload, his voice full of pain. "Damn shoulder's broke," he said. "Get up and give 'em the works."

I got up and gave 'em the works. The truck behind me was a jumble of corpses, in which one or two stirred weakly. I could half-see Pete on my right, and at least one soldier was still firing away on the left. The enemy was climbing in at us from saddles and from the ditch and once and again I had to step briskly back and fire from the hip as a contorted face topping a waving hand full of pistol came over the steel at me.

Then the gun was empty once more and this time I could not reload, for a wave of foemen, like pirates over a bulwark, swept across the side. Clubbing the weapon, I swept it around my head, bellowing hoarse oaths half-consciously. I knew I was done for and I wanted to take every man jack of them along with me to Hell.

The only crashes now were occasional pistol shots. We were all fighting with rifles and sub-machine guns clubbed. I felt that I was going down in a sea of arms, faces, and blue velvet; my arms ached, and my throat was parched and gritty. I was bloody...

I let the last man have a crack on the side of the head that catapulted him heels over head on a heap of carcasses, and by thunder, he *had* been the last, for suddenly I was standing alone!

The great ditch was a perfect charnel-house, with the undying horses struggling up its sides and single-footing it off toward the depleted main body, who had camped a long way off over the desert and hadn't made a move to back up this attack. There were wounded, though not so many as you'd expect, since most of the shooting had been very close range work indeed. I leaned over and killed a man who was screaming horribly, did it with a heavy crack on the head with the sub's butt; then looked for my comrades.

Pete Ashton, praise be, was alive, and climbing up from the ground to check on me. He'd been knocked over the side by some highwayman's onslaught. His only wound was a bruised back and head.

Kemp had a broken shoulder, a really wicked shatter, having been hit by a hurtling fellow and smashed against the truck. Two other soldiers had survived, both with minor gunshot wounds, I had a torn cheek (so had Pete from the first attack) and a nearly spent slug had gone through my shirt and broken the skin over my breastbone.

FIVE of us then were living. Perhaps six hundred highwaymen remained across the sand, if you included the women.

"Let's get back to the north side," said Kemp, wincing as he stood up. "Bandages and stuff over there." We all crossed the corpse-littered open space, in which a couple of horses stood silently, unmoving, left by their fellows; and we clambered into our first truck, and with small surprise I saw that Barbary was gone.

There was no sign of another sortie forming. Pete and I did what we could to help Kemp's shoulder—it was little enough, a matter of binding it in the most comfortable position, for we were no physicians, nor first-aid men either—and dabbed our own gashes with sulfa powder. As we finished, I heard a scratching at the truck-body, and reached out for a rifle. Barbary came over and slipped down onto the floor beside me.

"Where the hell were you?" I asked too amazed at her appearance to be intelligent.

She touched the diamond-headed hairpin thrust into her front curls. "Were out finding this chiv, cully, and putting some good fellows out o' their pain," she said. There was blood on her skirt, drying in very thin streaks where she'd wiped the bodkin after stabbing heaven knows how many of her countrymen. I knew it had been mercy on her part, but how cold, how cold a mercy!

And yet she did not repel me. She was a child of her wretched civilization, and probably not many of her fellow camp followers would even have bothered themselves to kill an agonized man out of pity.

"Why'd you come back?" I asked her.

She looked at me straight. "I gave you my word," she said. From a modern man it would have been sheer ham. From this fantastic, lovely anachronism, it was simple truth.

I think that was when I rose above my infatuation with her gorgeous body, and began to fall really in love with her.

CHAPTER ELEVEN

WE waited through the afternoon, and no attack materialized.

I could not think myself into the abstruse mind of Galloping Jonas, so I did not know whether he was appalled at his losses, or merely waiting till dark to launch a final attack, which must inevitably succeed, even against our vastly superior weapons.

At any rate, long before he was ready to do anything, there came an interruption that was first terrifying, and then horrible...

I had quite forgotten that beyond this trench and this flatland was an uncounted mass of allies. In the hills were a regiment of soldiery under a colonel as tough and smart as they come. Beyond these was America. Yet in the past hours I had not once thought of them. They were over the invisible wall, and my only problems were the girl and the dead horses and the living, inimical, out-of-joint high-waymen. Kemp and Pete and I fought in a tiny steel fortress, which might as well have been a million miles off the earth, for all we could expect help.

So when Pete suddenly gripped my arm and pointed up and out, and I saw the airplane heading straight for us, I could not believe my eyes. I could not even think for a moment what the flying thing was. On it came, and Kemp saw it too and said sourly. "Well, so much for us."

"Huh!" I said, frowning.

"That's the biggest bomber you ever saw, mister, and it's coming to lay an egg on us. Old Uncle may not know what's keeping his ground troops out of here, but he sure as hell's not gonna let a bunch of idiots on horses ride all over this ditch lookin' at military secrets forever." He spat. "Relax," he said as Pete jumped to his feet, "you'll never feel it. Though damn it," he added, almost wistfully, "I sure would have liked to see what made them horses tick. No time now. We got maybe thirty seconds."

I did the first, the most important thing that occurred to me. I rolled over once and came beside Barbary and took her in my arms and kissed her as hard as I could.

I was wholly surprised to find her returning my kiss.

I was even more surprised to find in what must have been more than 30 seconds that I was still alive and able to appreciate her lips, I turned and looked up. At that instant the bomber, flying at a height of at least two miles, exploded. We could not hear the sound, but the vivid glare hurt our eyes, and moments later we felt the shock through the earth.

"Good Lord," said Kemp, actually shaken, "it hit the wall!"

They didn't send any more bombers that day.

AFTER a while Pete got out the red book, which I'd taken from Barbary, and we pored over it. It was an amazing volume. Down the left side of each page (it was printed on strange, parchment-like paper, bound in velvet) ran a series of squiggles, a little like Arabic writing, a little like kitten tracks in whitewash, a little like Egyptian hieroglyphs. Down the right side were ranked English words in old-style type. On the first page I read, "jazy, crib, fambles, eye (or glim), run…"

"It's a dictionary," said Pete, quite tremulous with excitement. "Look, the first character's the same for all these hen-prints. *Jazy* used to mean *wig*. It's like a French-English lexicon; only what kind of impossible French is that?"

"Nothing we ever heard of," I said. An idea took me. I snatched the book and thumbed through till I found the word "oil." Then I shoved it under Barbary's nose, pointing to the scribbly characters opposite "oil." "Does that say *zaminfler?*" I asked her.

She read, and for a while she could not speak, and then she stammered, "No, it s—says *fufre.*" If I ever laid eye on a girl who was paralyzed with awe, it was Barbary in that moment.

"Then *zaminfler* is gas?"

"Gasses. The s-s-singular is *zimbander.*"

"What lingo? What tongue, language—"

"You wouldn't know it if I told ye, cully."

"It's not a language of this world," said Pete, with no questioning in his voice, but a chill certainty; and the woman said, "You're right, but how ye knew, bowman, flogs me."

"Why shouldn't we know?"

"Why, ye can't have been here long enough yourselves to learn every speech in the planet!"

"What? We were born here."

"Go on!" she said. Well, it wasn't quite that, but an obscene and derisive phrase meaning that. "Did ye or did ye not send a ship through the air at a speed faster than light's and only a matter of days ago? And do ye tell me, cream-face, that you were born here on Earth?" Then she sat back, opening her great eyes wide. "Wait, now, this is 1963?" We nodded, fascinated. "Then you might have been born here, o' course. When did your fathers, or ancestors, land? And from where?"

"My ancestors landed in 1693 from England," I said.

Her mobile face expressed seven or eight emotions, and then settled into disbelief. "You sit there in those silly clothes, having passed the speed of light with an airship, having killed my friends with weapons like Earth never saw, and yet ye swear you are of Earth. I'd begun to like you, but I'm plagued if I'll take up with a liar so huge, so black-tongued…"

I shook the wench till her head rattled. "See here, Barbary," I said, "there are five of us here and one of you, and before we tell you any more facts you won't believe, suppose you just explain yourself, and your companions, to us."

"Takes five bullies to whip one girl, eh?"

"No, no; majority rules, that's all."

She laughed. The essential good nature of the girl overcame her. "All right, cully. Ask away."

"Where are *you* from?"

"Another world. Another planet. Far away from here, and I won't say where, 'cause you'd send word to *your* planet and they'd attack mine—"

"As we don't have another planet, that's balderdash; besides, why would we attack you?"

"Cly off the poplars of yarrum!" she bawled out, which I took to be an exclamation of amazement, because her jaw dropped and she shook her head. "Ye've just murdered hundreds upon hund—"

"Galloping Jonas started that; he shot Captain Granville. Your precious pals have been holding up stages—I mean busses and trains—all over the West. Several times that tall blond bastard all but shot me in cold blood. Did you expect us to sit quietly—on our sand dunes and wait to be cut down one by one?"

"Why not?" she asked, honestly startled. "It's his business to shoot people; he's a royal scamp, a highway leveler, a rogue o' the King's highway. The highwayman is king of mankind, and can do as he pleases."

"Maybe on your world, but not this one."

"Man, man, do ye not try to lie so outrageously to me, for I know more than you think! There are no highwaymen on my world, but on this, there are thousands, and their business is to kill and rob and carouse. As mine is to please them."

"And do you?" I asked, jealousy gnawing at my brains.

"I haven't begun yet, for there are arguments as to whose doxy I'll be. So I'm yet a dell." I hoped I had that last word figured out right. I hesitated to ask her. She went on: "I don't know where you're from, for so far as we know there's none among all the habitable planets of the universe whose people have sped past light itself, save us. Would ye tell me? To please dear Barbary?" She was directing this outrageous attempt at me. By thunder, if we'd been alone, it would have had me purring.

"Babe," Kemp said suddenly, "you are a total wack, and for two cents I'd shoot you like a snake. But I think you're really from some damn other place, and lemme tell you in plain words, we live here, we've always lived here, and we always will. Until your boy friends plow us under, I mean."

"There's one without the intellect to lie," said Barbary, doing Kemp an injustice. "Can this be true?"

"Certainly it's true."

"Then why don't ye know that highwaymen are the kings of men? Why do ye dress so oddly and lack horses, and where did ye get these metal carts and how, how, *how* did ye surpass light's speed?"

I took the last query first. "We discovered a metal and a fuel that enabled us to do that this year."

She had me repeat it. Blinking, she asked several questions that, although she was limited to an 18th-Century vocabulary, still were keen and basically scientific in thought. Then she pled with me for a while to think, and being tired of all the idiotic back-and-forth nonsense, I said okay. She sat down in a corner of the hot truck by herself, and gazed at her feet, muttering.

Slowly the sun sank, and vanished, and dusk came on the desert; and still there was no sign of attack from the distant flat where Galloping Jonas camped with his merry men.

CHAPTER TWELVE

WHEN she came to me in the fading light, she was humbled and friendly and worried; almost, I thought, apologetic.

"Cully—what's your name? Sam? Sam love, you bussed me a bit ago, and 'twas an honest, passionate clip, and I enjoyed it. I must tell you, I like ye better than ever I've liked Jonas. But I feel something terribly wrong, and I even think 'tis not with you, but with us, or mayhap the world we're on," She bit her lips, considering. "Do you answer me this, Sam honey: did I understand you to say that ye've passed the light barrier *for the first time?*"

"That's right."

She wrestled with it as with an incredible conception. "First," she murmured, "First time. Heavens! Can such a thing be?" Her eyes turned their full glorious force on me. "If there is one almighty rule of the universe," she said solemnly, "tis this... What is, was, and will be. There are new things to people, to individuals, but not to nations and worlds. How can there be? Things have always been the same.

"Listen again, Sam. On my world there are no highwaymen, no horses, nothing new. A thing is new to a child, but any adult must know everything in his world and cannot find anything new. Unless, mark ye, he goes to another world. On your planet, there are supposed to be highwaymen, horses, little science and less civilization. Yet here we've come to it, prepared to meet its conditions; prepared from our births to be highwaymen, prime ministers, and doxies, which are the greatest beings of this planet. And here are you, like great men from another planet yourselves, and atop this, you've done something we have always done, and yet *for the first time.*"

I grappled with this hodgepodge and deciphered it slowly. "You came here in space ships." I said slowly.

She nodded and quietly said, "Aye."

"You were prepared to infiltrate—to merge with us, thinking to rule us, to observe us from vantage places of enormous power and importance," Again she said yes. "Then your people have been here before!"

"Yes, in the 18th Century. They hid and studied, and kidnapped people of England to take home to our world. For nigh three hundred years we prepared—I mean my people, for heaven knows I myself am only twenty-years old, Earth years—and the ancestors of all our band were chosen and bred to produce offspring who looked exactly like your own folk." I wondered if the usual people on her world were less human than she and Jonas. I dared not ask. "The horses were manufactured. Heavens, that took 150 years itself."

"And then you forgot to make them breathe," So the nags were complex and clever machines! Man alive, but *that* explained a lot!

"Aye, I guess they did forget. So anyway when all was ready, we came, and landed, though in America by an error rather than England, and found—you know what we found. We were upset, baffled and—"

"Afraid?" I suggested when she paused.

SHE flashed out at me, "No! We're bred to fear nothing, as is the heritage of the highwaymen!"

"Baby," I said, "when those scouts of yours studied the England of 1725, they took a lot of romantic talk and horse-leavings as gospel truth. The highwaymen were called kings of mankind, but they weren't, they were scum, and only the romantics of the time thought them otherwise. And in addition, this will bowl you over, but there was and is only *one* Prime Minister."

"Now you're lying again!" An angry hand crept toward the diamond pin in her hair. I shook my head, chuckling, and I think she believed me at last. "Someone made awful mistakes then, and when we go home their graves'll be dug up and their bones spat on," she said, with a couple of choice cuss words.

"Your people may be wizards at science, but they sure make boners by the basketful," said Pete Ashton, who had been listening silently behind us. "There's one thing I don't get; did you really think that when you came back in 250 years that things would be precisely the same as they were then?"

"O' course we thought so. What is, was, and will be."

"Sam," said Pete, "I get what the young lady's trying to impart. Their race has absolutely no conception of progress. They believe that if you can break the light bar-rier today, you could have done it last year, or last eon. They must have been stabilized so long ago that beginnings are lost in antiquity. They simply don't comprehend ad-vancement. The status quo was always quo and always will be quo, if I may make a bon mot. Such a state of affairs is admissible to me, but I gather that the opposite isn't true. It isn't possible to their minds that a son can know more and be able to do more than a father."

"True," said Barbary, "he can't. How can it be otherwise?"

"They laughed at Fulton," said Pete absently. "We have some of that same feeling right here on Earth. Thank the powers, we don't have it to any such ridiculous lengths!"

"D'ye see why I'm all aflutter?" asked Barbary. "D'ye take my confusion? There are things here that cannot be! Where are the horses, and whence came this monstrosity we're sitting in?"

I tried to tell her how it was, I presumed a primitive civilization on her own world; described how they must have found out the secrets of the atom, of science, and then come at last to a place where no advance was made; and after centuries, centuries and tens of centuries, of absolute stand still, the history was forgotten (perhaps it had never been written at all) and the race came to believe things had always been this way. It was an alien concept to me, but I could grasp it. She could not grasp ours, though. It was like a savage trying to understand the Trinity; yet this girl and her people were technically at least a thousand years ahead of me!

She did not understand, but she did come to believe me, for the evidence of Earth's progress was too patent to deny. And she clapped a hand to her mouth at last and gasped, "Ah, the terrible thing we've done, then, murdering and all, when 'tis not your way! When the highwayman is truly not the king!"

"Why, your own people don't murder, then?" asked Pete.

"No! We're civilized. But we learned to do it, we who were born to come here, because it was said 'twas the thing the great ones did. All those deaths for nothing! I must go and explain to Jonas."

But it was too late to explain anything to Galloping Jonas. From the desert came the bark of a pistol, and then a high voice out of the darkness. I had not realized it had grown so black around us. The moon was not quite up, and the land was shrouded and full of dim shapes. The voice cried. "Ye rapparee buffers in there! Jonas' compliments, and will ye now prepare yourselves, for ye'll be dead within the half hour!"

Barbary screamed out something in a language I could not understand—I presumed it was her native tongue—but her shrill call was deadened and ignored, as half a thousand horses got into motion, and the sands echoed under their flailing hooves.

The last attack had begun.

CHAPTER THIRTEEN

THE main body was still a good distance off, and evidently the voice that had called, after the signaling shot, must have been that of an advance scout. We had a minute or two at most, and I thought faster than I'd thought since the day Pete and I were caught in the girls' dorm, back in sophomore days.

"Listen," I said rapidly, "if we can sucker them into the ditch, and get down to the launching platform, the ship's ready for another test flight—"

"Oh, brother!" said Pete. "Let's go."

"But we've got to decoy them into the ditch." I knew that the trucks would explode like shrapnel bombs when the tiny rocket plowed through them, and I remembered that we'd found the oiled paper screen all over an acre of desert. "At least we've got to get them damn close to it," I added.

"I'll sucker them for you," said Kemp in the darkness. "I'll stay here and make 'em think there's forty of us left. Get going."

"Don't be an ass," said Pete. "Do you know what'll happen when the ship comes down this channel at better than 190,000 miles per second?"

"I know I won't feel it. And I know I'm sick of listening to all this damn chatter, and you'd better get to running, because I'm gonna spray this truck with Thompson slugs in just twenty seconds. And I ain't kidding, buster," said Kemp.

I thought maybe he'd gone out of his head with the pain of his shoulder. I would have moved at him, but I somehow knew that he wasn't joking about the sub-machine gun. I handed Barbary over the north side of the truck, as Pete and the two soldiers jumped to the concrete. Then, as I was climbing over myself, trying to think of something to say. Kemp gave a small hard bark, I realized it was a laugh.

"I wouldn't have done it, mister. But look, I'm all mucked up inside. It ain't only the shoulder, my whole chest is shoved in. I ain't got but a couple days to go anyhow, so what the hell?" He choked. I believed he was telling the truth. Risking all our lives, I hung on a minute and said, "You're a good one, Kemp."

"You're a pretty fair boy yourself with that rifle. Hurry up. And kiss the babe for me!"

I was running down the black ditch, holding Barbary's arm as we stumbled along, and Kemp's words went round and round in my mind until suddenly the significance of one of them hit me. *Rifle.*

We had left every weapon we had back there in the trucks. Except of course, for Barbary's diamond bodkin.

WELL, spilled milk, what the hell. If the spaceship miniature wasn't enough to do the trick, we were just dead ducks anyway. I ran as hard as I could, and the wound in my backside opened up again and panged in pain as it had when I'd run down this stretch after Barbary so much earlier that day. The roar of galloping horses (I still could scarcely take in the fact that they were mechanical things; how did they work?) was laced now by the chatter and stammer of Kemp's machinegun. Too great a range, I thought, and realized that he was creating the illusion of a great number of defenders. A rifle spoke then, and a short burst of machinegun fire, and again the rifle.

"For a man with a shattered shoulder," Pete panted, "he's doing magnificently."

"He is a great guy," said one of the soldiers. It was the first time I'd heard him speak. It kind of shocked me. I don't know why. I guess I'd been thinking of our party as Pete and Kemp and Barbary and me. "He'd have made a good sergeant," said the soldier. I thought Kemp could have had no finer epitaph.

We reached the end of the trench, the launching platform loomed square and strangely homey before us. The moon was rising, and objects became less murky. "Get the cover off," said Pete.

"Oh no—it's locked."

"Break it." I broke the plastic with my fingernails, turning them back and tearing several in the process. There was the little ship, its small nose aimed down toward the cradle, twenty miles off.

I knew the workings of it. I slaved, feverish, fumbling, and terribly afraid of what I had to do. It wasn't the extraterrestrial invaders, for they'd asked for it; it was Kemp. Nevertheless there was a menace, not only to Pete and me, and our world, but to Barbary, who was a woman and whom I loved. And Kemp had said he couldn't last long.

I couldn't rid myself of the guilt horror, but I worked on, and finally was ready; and still Kemp's gun crashed and stuttered, and pistols barked back over the sand.

Now the horses were silent. Now they had come to the edge of the trench and were pouring in afoot. Now I was ready.

Kemp's gun stopped.

I hoped he was dead, I believe that he was, probably with a merciful bullet in the brain from a great antique horse pistol manufactured on another planet far out in space.

"Get down," I told Pete. He held Barbary below the level of the great reinforced-concrete-and-steel sheltering screen. The soldiers ducked beside him.

I did what was necessary, and at 190,000 miles a second the tiny missile shot down toward its haven.

There was the most ungodly blast anyone ever heard. To this day I carry a souvenir of that sound, in abnormally sensitive eardrums. It was as though an A-bomb blast zone had ended just two hundred yards from my nose.

No other sound could penetrate that blast and its vast echoes. Lying flat on my face, praying and full of a terror like nothing I'd ever known, I waited; and seconds, or years, later, the whine of flying metal, and the screams of tortured men came through to me.

The trucks had indeed gone up like a charge of TNT. The ship alone would have slain everyone in the ditch, simply by its passing. The barricade of machines accounted for those who were on the desert around it.

When I was sure that no more shards of steel were slicing through the air, I got up and stared out over the moonlit desert. Nothing moved near the ditch. With a word of caution to Barbary and the others, I walked down toward the place where we had so lately been fighting.

THE carnage was awful. There was very little sound now, only a creak as a piece of metal cooled or fell over, or perhaps a sigh as a man expired. I guess I was looking for Kemp, which was stupid, for we'd never find anything identifiable as the corporal.

There were two horses lying together, back from the rim of the ditch a ways. I went toward them, because they were the first of the artificial chargers I had seen off their feet. I bent to examine them, saw that hide and hair were torn, exposing dull green metal framework and beyond that, machinery of a complex and recondite appearance.

Torn from the horror I had created, fascinated despite myself by these miracles of craftsmanship, I knelt beside them and began tugging away the hide (synthetic too) and the broken inner frame to get at the works. And for this curiosity I nearly died.

I didn't hear him come at me; I only missed getting the dirk between my shoulders because I leaned sideways to reach for a sprocketed wheel to use as a lever. I didn't even hear the rush of air as his lean blade whistled down. I only knew he was there when a trail of fire slid from the nape of my twisting neck down along my clavicle, and the arm of the attacker struck me simultaneously on the back.

I hurled myself farther to the side, thus missing a chance to grab his arm; but it was too sudden to give me an instant to think. Turning as I fell, I lashed out with one foot and by luck caught him on the knee so that he staggered back, cursing, and gave me time to get on my feet. Then, in the split second before he sprang on me, I saw that he was the fat moldy butterball of a rogue, Gothic Beall.

I underrated him. I poked at his face as he leaped, thinking that a sock in the nose would stop him, he looked so soft and sloppy. Not he! That plump frame hid muscles of whalebone. My wallop glanced off, and his dirk thrust for my chest. Only a perfect cat-spring of a jump saved me from death, as I went backward and just had my shirt touched by the blade.

Off balance, all I could do was flail wildly for his arm and catch it, and try my best to hang onto it, as he followed me back; then, staggering further, my calves hit the broken apparatus that had been a "horse." Down I went, and again pain reminded me fleetingly of Barbary, as my wound crunched on a spring or some other gadget that protruded upward. Good Lord! Even the prospect of death couldn't keep me from flinching, relaxing my grip on Beall's arm, and clapping my hand to my seat. And Beall, with a whoop of dismal glee, slashed out and got me on the forehead, a long, superficial gash that poured blood into my eyes at once.

I did a complete backward somersault. Only muscles toned by long hours of work on the flat furrow allowed me to do it without breaking my neck. My whipping heels caught him somewhere, I think on the jaw; for when I had come to my feet beyond the horse, and wiped blood from my eyes with one hand while groping out blindly to ward off blows with the other, I saw him sitting a yard or two off, shaking his head. I went for him as he bounded upright again.

We closed, and like knife-brawlers of the last century, caught one another's wrists and heaved and panted and struggled with great ferocity. We lashed out at each other with our toes, and tried to trip the enemy, and worked our way around the sands in short, stumbling jerks of motion. There was no question that he was the strongest man I had ever tangled with; his short arms bulged with massive lumps of muscle, cords stood out on his thick neck as he heaved and called me foul names in his synthetic 18th-Century speech.

And slowly, slowly, I bent back his wrist, and slowly brought the dirk round so that, sweating horribly, he saw it come near his own chest; and he dropped it, and so I shifted my grip to his throat, and angrily, savagely yet almost sadly, I killed him with my naked hands.

CHAPTER FOURTEEN

"BY Tyburn Tree!" said a loud, guttural voice, as I stood over Beall's carcass, heaving for breath. I looked, wiping more thin blood from my eyes, and there stood Galloping Jonas, twin pistols trained rigidly on my head. "By the dismal hole of Newgate, cully, but ye did that featly! As good a throttling as ever I clapped peeper to!"

I thought there was a change in the tall ruffian's voice—astonished, that the cant words and queer oaths had a decidedly hollow ring to them, as if his heart wasn't in it. And when he shoved the weapons into his belt, I knew that something was feeding on him so that the heart was out of his masquerade. I said, "You've made a mistake, Jonas, you and your friends from the other planet. I've talked to Barbary and she understands a little of it. There are no highwaymen here, and you're not king of men."

"Aye," he said slowly, "I grow 'ware of that, there's all kinds of hell brewing here."

"There were highwaymen in the old days," I told him, "but there are none left today." He regarded me dully, and I knew he didn't understand it any better than Barbary had at first. So I tried to tell him in a simple way he could grasp. "Your scouts made a mistake back in 1725," I said. It was progress—not error—that his race could not conceive. "We are far beyond the primitive state you were prepared to meet, Jonas. We can send ships faster than light—"

"Aye!" he said nodding, "I know. Our devices told us that some days ago, which is why we headed this way, to reconnoiter and find what had gone amiss."

"You've been fighting out of sheer bewilderment," I said and he agreed with a shake of the head. "And because of the nature bred into you, too."

"Ye know of that?"

"Barbary told me."

"Is the wench dead?"

"No. She's safe."

"I'm glad," he said. "I love the doxy… Well," he said, more loudly, and a hint of the old ire coming into his voice, "I reckon I should gun ye for what ye did to Beall, and to my poor lads here." He waited a minute, thinking. "There's no profit in it," he said finally. "Twas our mistake. We'll leave, what's left of us. Go back to your pals. I'll lift the wall and go."

"That wall," I said, "is it a force field?" His strange rudimentary sense of English meanings grappled with that, and he replied, "I think that's close to it; I think it's fairly close; I know it not in your tongue."

"Can you get back to your ships?"

"Easily. And mark me, hick, when we've studied this out, we'll come again, and next time ye shan't know us, but ye'll buckle under to us."

I had my doubts of that, but kept silent; and as if remembering the exit lines of a play he was committed to act through, he shook himself and grinned evilly, and swept off the great black cocked hat and made me a formal bow. "Your servant, sir, and do ye go free with the compliments of Galloping Jonas, who bids ye give thanks to your gods that he is a forgiving and a merciful knight of the road!"

Then he was gone, or so I thought, into the shadows of the desert night; but as I turned, his voice came back to me again.

"Do ye send the girl Barbary out to us, though, or I'll ride in and carve all your weasands!"

I went back to Pete and Barbary and told them what had happened. Barbary kissed me on the mouth, a hot and promising kiss, and then without a word she had gone too; and I was quite, quite alone with a dreary, penetrating sorrow in my guts, for all the dead men and for the lovely dell that was born in another part of the universe.

When sleep came I had strange dreams of Barbary in her green velvet gown. She was standing on the edge of a precipice. The next moment she flung herself into the wind, soaring away into the sky. There were bizarre images of her in the grip of strange mechanical monstrosities. I screamed and felt the helplessness of being unable to rescue her. Later I dreamt of her in my arms on a distant plain, surrounded by tall flowers billowing in the wind. Her golden hair blew into my face. This was followed by moments of searing passion...

CHAPTER FIFTEEN

WE had one more scare the next morning, when another bomber came toward our flatland; this time there was no invisible wall to keep it out, and it flew over as the four of us who survived were eating a cold breakfast down by the launching platform. I almost hoped it *would* drop its damn bomb...but the crew, seeing that nothing moved below them, evidently used their judgments, and did not let the thing fall. Half an hour later the colonel and every man of his regiment were riding in toward us.

We explained as best we could. If it hadn't been for the evidence of that force field, and the corroboration of all our story by the two GIs, Pete Ashton and I would probably be in some booby hatch today. However, the colonel believed us, and later; so did the government and the world.

Galloping Jonas and the remnant of his men, with their women and most of their horses, had decamped in the night, relieving the desert of its encompassing wall. Their future progress Pete and I could trace easily in the papers. I give you a few of the minor headlines which nobody but us (and maybe the wiser heads of government) connected with the extraterrestrial invasion:

DRESS SHOP BURGLARIZED, 100 NEW OUTFITS TAKEN...
EXCLUSIVE TAILOR CLAIMS FORTY SUITS STOLEN IN BROAD DAY...
WAVE OF CAR THEFTS HITS LAS VEGAS...

DICTIONARIES MISSING, SAYS BOOK SHOP...and three or four weeks later,

NO TRACE OF DOZEN MISSING PERSON'S IN FLAGSTAFF; YET EVIDENCE OF FOUL PLAY LACKING...

Pete put down the paper after he'd read the last item aloud. "They're on their way to outer space, I suppose," he said. "Just as some poor baffled devils out of Gin Lane and Rotten Row found themselves in 1725. Jonas and his boys, after walking around and observing superficially for a while in their stolen suits, and picking up some autos and God knows what else for study and duplication, have taken off for home." He laughed. "In one or two hundred years, we'll have another brief abortive invasion. They'll figure out who's the 'king of mankind' on Earth, and they'll come back as movie stars, and big league pitchers, and bald-headed golfers. They'll come roaring down the highways in 1963 autos, and our descendants will gape out of their private planes and wonder what on earth's happen-ed, just like we did last month when the highwaymen came. And after some fiasco which I can only remotely imagine, the lads will go home again, freshly bewildered and still not understanding progress, and prepare to return as—I don't know what."

"Why did they come at all?" I wondered aloud.

"Power? I don't know."

"Maybe it was boredom. The ghastly boredom of a whole planet for which there's nothing ever new unless they find it on another world."

"I guess that's as close a guess as any." He lit a pipe. "What a curious, slapdash pack they are. Find this planet in a million, but can't set down in England, where they were headed. Spend centuries manufacturing horses, and forget to make 'em breathe. Train people from childhood to be invaders; but they have to carry lexicons with them because they can't always remember the words."

"When they come next time, with their automobiles and their modern slang and the clothes that'll be outdated ten years from now. I'll bet a cookie they'll land in China or Tibet," I said.

"Sure. They'll never catch up. They'll never blend with humanity and rule us in secret, they'll always stand out like great big six-foot sore thumbs."

"What if they'd brought their own weapons with them this time?" I said, thinking of that for the first time. "We wouldn't have stood a chance against them. It was only their flintlocks and black powder that let us whip 'em."

"I doubt if they have weapons. I doubt if they make war. Barbary said they didn't kill people at home. It must be a very simplified culture they have, to let the status quo persist for centuries. And when they obviously believe that a couple of weeks' study of a country will allow them to learn everything about it, then it's plain their own civilization is essentially most fearfully simple indeed. They took any Earthman's word for fact, back in 1725, or they wouldn't have had—well, seventeen prime ministers, for instance."

"I wonder how they found Earth in the first place?" I mused. "They must be out all the time, crews of them exploring the galaxies. They implied that they were infiltrating other planets, too. Likely planets where the civilization's so backward that it hasn't changed either in centuries. Why, there must be humans, or humanoid forms, all over space!"

"I always figured there were," said Pete. "I always did read them science fiction magazines religiously."

I went out afterwards to look at the launching platform, where our little ship was set for its next test flight. Then in the evening I went for a lonely walk on the desert, as I did every day…mostly to think of Barbary. This sundown found me in the low foothills, and when I rounded a valley's end and saw the girl astride the horse, I thought for a minute that my imagination was working overtime.

It was Barbary, though; in a stylish frock, immodestly tucked up to let her sit the saddle. We stared at one another for a time, not speaking and at last she said hesitantly, "Well, cully, are ye glad to see me or no?"

I didn't tell her. I dragged her off that damn horse and proved it to her.

CHAPTER SIXTEEN

GALLOPING Jonas is long gone from our world. The second wave of invaders, scheduled for a year after the first, did not materialize, for Jonas went home and stopped them. Barbary and I expect that our grandchildren, perhaps, or our great great grandchildren, will be dealing with her home's next expedition.

Jonas had raised a fuss about Barbary staying, but my wife is a strong-willed girl, as I well know. I have twinges where I sit down, every time it rains...and she still wears that diamond-headed hairpin, though today in a more modern coiffure.

She retains both her inborn nature, which is remarkably simple and good, and her acquired habits of 18th-Century thought, which are wild, unpredictable, and fantastic.

Everyone wonders how I can keep a stable of four splendid horses on my salary. They never notice that the horses do not breathe, that there's never any feed in the stalls. They were my wife's dowry, from Galloping Jonas. She taught me to control them—it's done mentally—and the artificial beasts are a joy to us when we take them out in the mists of early morning and tear over the desert at fifty and sixty miles an hour.

Above our fireplace is a plaque, set with half a hundred old English gold coins, Barbary had them in her purse when she came back to me; I suspect she lifted them from Jonas. Numismatists have offered us a fortune for them, because of their mint condition. We can't sell, naturally.

They're counterfeit, perfect but false, stamped out on a press in a world that lies halfway across the void.

Occasionally my wife points out to me the distant star around which her home planet revolves. The fact that it is invariably a different star, well, this is only delightful proof that my girl is the child of her slapdash race, the pseudo-highwaymen, the people without progress; the cosmic bunglers.

THE END

BEWARE THE GOD-GLOBES...

There were many legends that spoke of Earth's glorious past. Legends that spoke of its vast, powerful nations and empires. Legends that spoke of its freedoms and greatnesses. But this was the future. A future now riddled with fear. A future now ruled by god-globes, as men gazed up fearfully at a buttoned sky…

Here is another fine science-fantasy tale from one of the more underrated authors of the glory days of science fiction digest magazines, Geoffrey St. Reynard.

ABOUT GEOFFREY ST. REYNARD

Geoffrey St. Reynard...

...was nom de plume of Robert W. Krepps, who had a steady career as a writer of science fiction, fantasy, and horror from the mid-1940s through the mid-1950s. Born in Pittsburgh, PA in 1919, he broke into the field of fantastic fiction in 1945 when one of his earliest tales, *Wink Von Ripple*, was picked up by Raymond Palmer's *Fantastic Adventures* pulp magazine. Over the next eleven years, Krepps churned out many enjoyable works, including two memorable short novels, *Beware, the Usurpers* and *Armageddon 1970,* both of which appeared in William L. Hamling's sci-fi/fantasy digest magazine, *Imagination*. Krepps was known for writing his fiction with his favorite classical music pieces blasting away in the background. After his short novel, *The Cosmic Bunglers,* appeared in 1956, Krepps left the sci-fi and fantasy fiction field. He passed away at the ripe old age of 80 on January 24th, 1980.

THE
BUTTONED
SKY

By
GEOFFREY ST. REYNARD

ARMCHAIR FICTION
PO Box 4369, Medford, Oregon 97501-0168

*For more information about Armchair Books and products, visit our
website at...*

www.armchairfiction.com

Or email us at...

armchairfiction@yahoo.com

CHAPTER ONE

The squire he sat in Dolfya Town,
He swilled the blood-dark wine:
"O who can blight my happiness,
Or face the power that's mine?"

Then up there spoke his daughter fair:
"The priest can end your joy;
The globe can sap your might away,
And the Mink can you destroy!"
    —Ruck's Ballad of the Mink

The day that Revel killed a god, he woke early. There was a bitter taste in his mouth, and a pain in his ear where somebody'd hit him during a shebeen brawl the night before. He rolled over on his back. The bed was a hollowed place in the earth floor, filled with leaves and dried grass and spread with yellow-brown mink skins sewn into a big blanket; he'd slept on it every night of his twenty-eight years, but this morning it felt hard and uncomfortable.

The water gourd was empty. In the cold gray mists of dawn he groped his way sleepily to the well behind the hut, and drew up the bucket.

"Damn the gentry!" he burst out. The bucket, an ancient thing made of oak slats pegged together with wooden dowels, was half filled with dirt and rotten brush. "Curse their lousy carcasses to hell!" he yelled, and, suddenly scared, looked around to see if perhaps a god was floating somewhere near him. But no yellow glimmering showed in the mists.

Laboriously he cleaned out the well, dropping the bucket time after time and dragging up loads of trash. Some roving band of gentry had fouled the water for sport. Anything that hurt the ruck, made them more work or injured them in any way, was sport for the squirarchy.

At last he got a bucket of cold and almost clean water, filled the big gourd and carried it back to the one-room hut. The morning that had begun badly was getting worse; his mother's limp was painful to see; she must have had a hard night. Bent and gray and as juiceless as the grass of their beds, she slept more lightly and fretfully with every passing month. Many years before a squire had ridden her down in the lanes of Dolfya Town, as she scurried out of the path of his great stallion, and her broken leg had mended crookedly. A few hours on the mink-covered bed crippled her up so that moving was an agony.

With the impious brain at the center of his skull—Revel had long before decided that he had a number of brains, one obedient, one rebellious, one dull, one keen and inquisitive, and so on—with the impious brain he now cursed the gods and the gentry and the priests, and everyone above the ruck who preyed on them and made their lives so stinking awful. If he had thought then of killing a god, the idea would have seemed pleasant indeed. But quite impossible, of course, for a man of the ruck did not touch a god, much less slay one.

He did not think of such a thing, but cursed the gods briefly and then turned off his impious brain and began to wolf down his food. He paid no attention to what he ate—it was the same old bread of wild barley seeds, the same old boiled rabbit.

When he finished, he glanced at his mother, feeling sorry for her, wishing that she would go to the shebeens with him and have at least a little happiness before she died. He wondered if she had ever known any joy, any hope such as he had in drunken flashes now and then of belief that life might some day be better for the ruck. He shook his head, grabbed his miner's pick, booted his brother in the ribs to waken him, and left the miserable hut to walk to the mine for his day's work.

The day was brightening, and above him in concentric circles to the horizon and beyond hovered the eternal red and blue buttons. He looked up grimly. Always there, in all the spoken history of man, stretched above the world to keep watch on every action of the ruck. The buttons were full of gods, omnipotent, omnipresent.

The mine was a mile from his hut, which lay on the outskirts of Dolfya. It was halfway down a long valley, a gut between hills pitted with many other mines. There coal was dug for the gentry and the priests. He walked up to the entrance, gave his name telepathically to the god-guard at the top of the shaft, and went down the ladders until he'd reached his level. Another god passed him there, its aura of energy just touching his skin and tingling it into small bumps.

Shutting off the thoughts of his various brains from any probing mind that might be eavesdropping, he said to himself, Always, always they're near a man! You go out of your hut and there's a god, a big golden globe hanging in the air shoving its tentacles at you and reading your mind. You come down the mine shaft and every hundred feet or so you see the yellow luminosity. Why can't they leave us alone! Why can't they stick to their temples, and exact their worship on Orbsday, instead of all week long, all day long, every day in the year!

He came to his work place, a dead-end tunnel. Jerran was there before him, as usual. Revel grinned at him. Jerran was a runty wisp of a man, with a face the color of old straw, and he had been Revel's friend since the day he came to the mine from distant Hakes Town by the sea. A wonderful drinking companion, Jerran, but he wouldn't brawl...strange! He was forever pulling Revel out of fights and trying to teach him serenity.

As Revel greeted him, he involuntarily glanced at the end of the tunnel. There, behind a carefully casual erection of boulders, lay their secret cave. They'd broken into it the morning before, and after no more than a hasty glimpse of unknown wonders, and a check to see that no globes were in sight, they'd walled up the opening and begun to dig along the shaft's sides. Revel wasn't quite sure why he had followed Jerran's lead in keeping it secret, but the brain which had decided to do it must be the rebellious one. All secrets were taboo to the ruck, who were required to report all finds to the gentry or the god-guards.

Now a globe came drifting down the corridor, and Revel got quickly to work, prying coal from a vein with his pick. The thing passed him, flicking his mind lightly with its own, and went on to the end of the tunnel. He watched it from the tail of his eye. Its glow brightened with interest; it shifted back and forth before the rampart of rocks.

They hadn't kept a tight enough check on their excitement yesterday! The globes could sense emotions long after the man who'd had them left a spot, and if the emotion were anger or grief or strong excitement, the globes could detect their residue as much as forty-eight hours later.

The thing floated back to them, briskly now, and ordered Revel telepathically to pull down some of the rocks at the end.

He eyed it coolly, his various brains walled with the protective screen that he had learned to erect between his thoughts and the outside world. This screen was made of shallow ideas, humdrum speculations on prosaic things— the last woman he'd had, the good feeling he got from working this rich vein of coal after some days of poor luck, even (to make the god think it was hearing secret desires) a wish that he might taste the wine that the gentry drank. He could throw up the screen and forget it, using his core of brains for serious plans.

A dozen rocks displaced, he thought, and we're doomed. For not telling the gods about the cave, he and Jerran would be given to the squires for the next big hunt.

So, without much hope of living through the next minute, but believing it was the only thing he could do now, he shoved Jerran to one side, raised his pick and slammed it with all his might into the center of the small, gold, eight-tentacled sphere.

And Revel had killed a god!

The feel of the pick slashing through it told him that: it was like hitting an overripe melon. The globe recoiled, dragged itself off the pick, and sank toward the floor, wobbling and dripping yellow ooze, with its aura of energy fading quickly into air. Jerran said quietly, "No others in sight. We're lucky!" and began to make a hole in a pile of discarded rocks. "Help me hide it, Revel."

"You can't hide it," he said dully. "They're telepathic, after all. It must have signaled its consorts."

"They can't hear or send messages through rock," said Jerran, working away. Revel automatically started to help him.

"How do you know?"

"We've proved it."

Revel heard the phrase, wondered who "we" might be; but so much had happened in the last seconds that he did not question Jerran. He couldn't absorb all the shattering facts. A man could not only touch a god, he could murder it! The gods were not all-powerful, for they could not perform telepathy if rock were in the way. Truly it was a morning of wonders. The world was falling around him.

He stared at the limp corpse of the globe. The tentacles were already shriveling up, the emanation of energy that surrounded the living orbs was gone. He bent, sniffed; no odor. He peered at it keenly, in the soft blue light of the mine's lanterns, then straightened.

A hand fell on his shoulder.

He spun on one heel, the pick arcing round to gut whoever was behind him. He had a glimpse of a short red beard and a popping walleye, and stopped his whirl by an instantaneous checking of his whole muscular system. The pick's point, still splattered with god's gore, was nudging his brother's belly.

"Nobody could have halted such a swing but you, Revel," said Rack absently. His good eye, ice blue and sharp as a bone needle, was fixed on the dead globe. "What happened?"

"An accident," said Jerran. "The god interposed itself between your brother's pick and the coal."

"That's right," said Revel. He had been lying to his brother for years, but he never grew reconciled to it; still, Rack was a man with but one brain, and that one servile and obedient to every whim of the gentry, the priests, the gods. So he had to be lied to.

Rack brought his gaze to Revel's tense face. "I got in the way of your pick," he said heavily. "You have the keenest nerves, the strongest body in the mines. This was no accident."

Revel began to grow cold in the head and the bowels. If Rack was convinced that he'd slain the god on purpose, then he'd report him. The religion that held the world so tightly was greater than any family bonds. He looked up at Rack. The man was a giant towering four inches over Revel's six feet one, and sixty pounds heavier. Rack's eyes were blue and white, Revel's lustrous brown; the elder's hair and beard were flame-colored, the younger had a sleek chocolate-brown thatch with a hint of rich black in its sheen, and was clean-shaven.

I'd hate to kill you, big man, thought Revel, but if I must, to save my neck, I will.

Jerran thrust his pick under the flaccid corpse and tossed it with one quick motion into the hole. He piled rocks on it, as Revel stamped the yellow ichor out thin and stringy, spread rock dust and jetty coal fragments over it till no sign of the murder remained.

"I'll report it," said Rack, apparently making up his mind.

"Then I'll say you did it," snapped Jerran, turning on him like a mouse baiting a bear. "What chance would you stand in the temple against me, whose cousin serves in the mansion of Ewyo of Dolfya?"

It was true, Jerran was slightly higher in the ruck than the brothers, being related to a servant of the gentry. Revel hoped Rack would be scared off by the threat. He had become perfectly cold now and could in the blinking of an eyelash bury his pick in Rack's head, but he didn't want to do it.

When Rack said nothing, Revel spoke. "Brother, agree to hold your tongue, or by Orb, I'll cut you down where you stand!"

Rack glanced at his own pick. "You could do it," he acknowledged. "You're fast enough. All right. I promise." He turned to his work stolidly; only Revel could see that he was blazing with anger.

The three began to dig coal from the wall. Revel kept glancing at the small Jerran. What was there to the man that he had never suspected? How did he know that globes were stymied by rock? Why had he taken the death of the god so lightly?

What was Jerran, anyhow?

CHAPTER TWO

The squire has gathered all his kin,
To hunt the fox so sly;
'Tis not a beast with paws and brush,
But a man like you or I!

They hunt him down the thorny glen,
And up the hillside dark;
"O hear him gasp and hear him sob,
Whenas our hounds do bark!"
    —Ruck's Ballad of the Mink

When Revel was due for a rest space, he went through the blue-tinged dusk of the mine, cleaned his arms and face at the washers, scrubbing the coal dust from his big hands, and climbed the ladders, up and up, till day shone in his face.

He stood beneath the cross-beam of the entrance, sucking in clean air. The red and blue buttons shone in the sun; far down the valley a globe passed between trees, bent on some private business. Another floated by him into the mine; under it trotted a zanph, one of the ugly beasts, six-legged and furry with the head of a great snake, that followed the globes and sometimes attacked men on orders from the hovering gods.

Would the deities discover that one was missing? If they found the corpse, he and Jerran would be foxes for the gentry...

Revel was a man of the ruck. The ruck was millions and millions of souls, faceless, without rights; Revel had some little protection, more than most others, being a miner and therefore important to the gentry. The gentry numbered thousands, and they had many rights—owning great estates, lighting their homes with candles, drinking wine legally, keeping fierce dogs and going where they pleased on big wild horses. No man of the ruck could touch one of the gentry and live. The gentry, the squires who owned guns and hunted men three times a week, men called "foxes"—it was whispered in the illegal drinking huts, the shebeens, that the squires had once been members of the ruck. Above there were the priests, who had always from the dawn of time been of the priestcraft, being born a notch lower than the gods themselves, who were the golden globes.

"Our Orbs who dwell in the buttoned sky," said Revel aloud, and spat. Before that day he wouldn't have dared to think of such an action.

He walked out on the shelf of rock before the mine. Something moved at the far end of the valley, a brown and silver speck that swiftly became a horse and rider, rocketing toward him.

It was a girl, her silver gown pulled up to the tops of her thighs so she could sit astride; she appeared to be having trouble with her mount. Passing beneath Revel, swearing loudly at the plunging horse, she continued for a hundred feet, then fell in a swirl of silver cloth as the brute reared.

Revel leaped down the rock shelf as the horse cantered away. He ran to the girl, who lay flat on her back, long white legs bared below the disordered gown. She was blonde, tall, beautifully slicked. No rucker wore such clothing, or rode a bay stallion, much less looked so groomed and cleanly; she was a squire's daughter.

As he bent down she opened eyes the shade of sunlight on gray slate.

"Lie still," he said, "you may have broken something, Lady."

Her face was scornful. "Stand back, miner," she said, recognizing his trade from the distinctive clothing he wore "Death to you if you touch me."

A confusion of emotions was rioting in him. So much had happened today—too much for sanity. He surrendered to madness gladly. This was the most perfect wench he had ever seen. "Shut up," he said, and ran his fingers over her body. "We of the ruck are expert at mending things, Lady: bones, pots, and lives. Orbs know, you gentry have busted enough of 'em for us. That hurt?"

She sat up, brushing her gown to her ankles as Revel took a last wistful look at her legs. Evidently she was quite unhurt. "You'll play fox for my father's hunt," she said coldly. "What made you do it?"

"You took a bad fall," he said lightly, wondering at his lack of fear. Never before had he touched a squire's woman. She felt as all women feel, her high caste couldn't be sensed in her body. "I'd sit still a moment, if I were you." It must be the killing of the globe, he thought; after that, any crime is possible.

"Who are you?"

"A miner," he mocked, standing. His pick was in his hand, as ever. He thought, Should I kill her too? No sense to that, when I was only trying to help. Or was it her body I wanted to touch? "Who's your father?"

"Ewyo of Dolfya, and his hounds will eat you for breakfast tomorrow."

Ewyo was one of the richest squires in this part of the world, and Jerran's cousin served him. "You're Lady Nirea, then. A fine-looking wench."

"My Orbs," she gasped, her scorn rattled by his incredible insolence. "My Orbs above, who are you?"

"A dirty miner, who puts coal into your father's hearth but must warm himself over smoldering peat. Why would you report me?"

"You *scum*," she said, the snarling hiss of a zanph in her voice. "Do you remember when a brewer fell over a dog in Dolfya last year and bumped my sister Jann? He was hunted over twelve miles before the pack tore him to blood and rags! What do you think *you* deserve, who dares address me in that way, and—and fondle me?"

"Lady Nirea, if I fondled you, you'd know it," Revel said. Then, seeing the hint of a smile on her sensuous lips, he looked up, for she seemed to be staring over his shoulder.

From the button above them a line of globes dropped, golden globules radiating bright energy.

Whom the gods destroy, they first madden. That was part of the Globate Credo, wasn't it? Well, Revel had been gradually made mad that day, and now, by Orbs, he'd show them something before he was destroyed!

As the first descended past him, and wrapped two tentacles under the girl's armpits to lift her, he lifted his pick to smack it as he had the supervising deity in the mine. He felt a tug; another globe had a whiplash arm around his pick. Gritting teeth, he threw his tremendous brawn into a swing, and the pick tore loose from the tentacle and sprayed the guts out of the sphere before him. It fell on the grass beside Nirea, an emptying sack. He slashed a second and a third, laughing between set lips. What a way to go down—killing gods!

Then he felt a searing pain, a sudden spasm of the flesh, as though a sword had been heated in a bonfire and laid alongside his ear. Reflectively he ducked to earth, sprang two steps forward and spun, rising to his full height again. One of the bulbous brutes had touched the side of his head, its energy aura so strong at that close contact that the hair was burned to a char and the flesh scorched.

So they could really hurt a man! He grinned with pain and defiance. If his pick wasn't as fast as any damned floating ball, let them kill him! He waited, crouched, keeping his eyes on them; and then they were rising again, leaving him there in the valley with a screaming girl in a silver gown.

Jerran, who had just started his own rest space, evidently, appeared on the rock shelf and came down, walking faster than Revel had ever seen him go. The little man came to him and, hardly glancing at Lady Nirea, said, "Were you attacked, lad?"

"I did the attacking, when they objected to my touching this wench."

Jerran gazed up. "They're spreading out. The gentry will soon be on you, Revel. You've got to hide."

"Where can you hide from a god?" It wasn't a hopeless tone he used, but a kind of laughing, bantering acceptance of his doom.

"Come off it," said Jerran urgently. "You're still thinking like a rucker."

"I am of the ruck."

"You're a rebel now, you fool! Think like one! Listen: *a man cannot kill a god.*"

"The Globate Credo," grunted Revel. "*Our Orbs are everlasting, untouchable.* Crud! I've killed four today."

"Right. So stop fearing them and thinking they're omnipotent. *Our Orbs see all we do.* More crud, lad! They're telepathic, adept at hypnosis, but rock stops 'em. Get rock above you and you are safe for a while, till I can think this over and get you some help."

"The mine!" Revel barked; to his madness, his exhilaration, was added hope. "The secret cave, Jerran!"

"And of course," said Jerran wryly, "you have to take the woman."

Revel's jaw dropped. "Why?"

"You idiot, she just heard you say about six words too many. She'd lead her father's pack straight to us!" Jerran evidently knew the Lady Nirea by sight. "She knows our names, too. It's either take her or kill her." His flinty eyes creased up. "Better kill her, at that. Less danger."

Revel looked at her. The talk of murder didn't turn a hair of that flawlessly-wrought coiffure: she was either too sure of the gentry's power, or too stunned by the gods' death, to be consciously frightened.

She was not stunned, for now she said, "You rabbit-brains, you filthy grubbers, you must have lost whatever wits a rucker has. My father will really think up something f—"

"Damn your father," said Jerran. "He eats dandelions."

"He doesn't!"

"My cousin gathers them for the old hellion," nodded Jerran. "I ought to know. Revel, have any of those bulbous bubbles gone into the mine, that you noticed?"

"Not yet, I've been watching."

"Good. Then get going. I'll take care of the wench."

Revel saw her lips curl slightly; she didn't believe she could be hurt, even though she had a moment before been screaming at the death of her gods. She was brave, or stupid, or very confident of her untouchability. He glanced down over her body, squeezed tight by the silver gown. Her breasts were fuller and higher than a ruck girl's, her limbs unbunched with muscles, smooth and lovely.

"No, she doesn't die," he said. "Not unless I do." He bent and picked her up and ran with her toward the entrance of the mine.

CHAPTER THREE

The Mink he couches underground,
Beneath the earth he lies;
He hears the fox's mournful yell,
And knows he must arise.

"Too many lads have hunted been,
Too many women slain!"
The Mink he takes his pick in hand
To end the gentry's reign.
    —Ruck's Ballad of the Mink

The Lady Nirea thought a moment—she never attacked any new problem without thinking beforehand—and then she began to struggle. This rucker who had her over his shoulder, with a death-grip on her legs and her head hanging down his back, was plainly insane. No man of his low position was *ever* insane enough to actually harm a squire's daughter; so if she kicked and bit, he would either drop her or—

Well, it was the "or." He reached up and slapped her on the rear. Hard. She opened her eyes wide. No one had ever before dared to touch her there. She thought again, and bit him on the side.

He was carrying her up the rocks toward the mine now. Surely there would be a god-guard on duty there? She had often seen one in place at the entrance, as she rode through the valley. Yes, peering upside-down under his arm, she saw the golden glow. Then he was shifting her a little, setting his muscles, and—great Orbs! He struck the god full in the middle with his miner's pick. This man, this astounding brute with chocolate-colored hair and a body like a wild woods lion, had dared kill four gods in as many minutes. Perhaps she shouldn't be as certain of her inviolability as she'd been till now.

"You triple-damn fool," she said, making her voice husky so it wouldn't squeak, "the globes are watching."

"They always are." What a strong voice the beast had.

"They see you going into the mine. D'you think you're safe here?"

"Where I'm going, there's a chance," he said. His body moved lithely beneath her. She clutched him around the ribs as they began to descend a ladder. Blackness, tinged with blue, lay below. She felt her scalp prickle with terror.

The little man, Jerran, said from somewhere above, "Kill all the gods we meet, lad; I'll hide or bring the bodies. And keep your emotions controlled, or they'll follow our scent like zanphs on the trail of a runaway."

"Did the globes follow us?" asked the big man, whose name was Rebel or something like it.

"They were coming down again as I ducked in. Hurry it up."

The swift plunge into the mine speeded. She deliberately worked herself up to silent panic, giving the gods a spoor to chase.

Now they were traveling on the level, and from the reflection of yellow, the brisk jerk of his arm, and the pulpy squish, she knew he had met and slain another globe. Was he inhuman, a visitor from beyond the world, such as were told of in the ancient ballads? Certainly no man was ever this bold!

"Here's the end," said Jerran. "Set the wench down, she can't get away. Hurry!"

She was rudely plumped onto a pile of coal. She looked at her silver gown and shuddered. Her flailing legs had ripped it from hem to midthigh; the coal was staining it irrevocably.

"When I catch that horse," she thought, half aloud, "I'll beat him. Tossing me into all this!"

They were pulling down rocks from the wall; now a black hole appeared. The small man jumped up to a boulder and snatched down a blue mine lantern. "Take this, Revel." That was it, Revel. An odd name, a rather nice one. The ruck ordinarily had such awful names, Jark and Dack and Orp. Revel. Not bad. It fitted the big lusty-looking brute.

He came over. "Never mind picking me up," she said icily. "I can walk." She peered into the hole, winced, and clambering over the rocks, losing a heel from one of her slippers, she entered their secret cavern.

Revel climbed in after her. Jerran was already piling rocks back into the breach. The lantern looked faint and incapable of lighting a chimney corner, but its blue radiance was deceptive, for the farthest reaches of the place were cast into a moonlight sort of glow. She gazed around, unable to take it in, seeing nothing at first but giant shapes of mystery, unknown things in stacks and in tumbled heaps, figures like grotesque statues, all lined in rows the length and breadth of the giant cavern.

The cave itself was square, perhaps a hundred feet to a side. It must have taken scores of miners months of work to hew it out of the rock. Unwilling to show interest, she still had to ask, "When did you make this?"

"We didn't make it, Lady. We found it. No man alive made this place."

"How do you know?"

"The miners would know it. We broke through the wall only yesterday."

"What are these things?"

"You know as much as I do." He was looking at her in the way her father sometimes looked at rucker serving women, as though she had no clothes on at all. She had little modesty, society was lax when it came to such things as clothing, and frequently she had ridden the streets of Dolfya Town in a suit of transparent silk that made the ruck gape and blush; but this very personal scrutiny made her shield her breasts with one arm as she stared back at him.

"I've changed my mind about you," she said pleasantly.

"Yes?" Did the swine look eager?

"I have...you won't be hunted by the pack. You'll be flayed alive, inch by inch, with white-hot needles of iron, starting with your feet and working upward. And I'll watch."

He laughed. "You *are* a wench," he said admiringly. Then he turned and appeared to forget her as he began to inspect the contents of the cavern. After a moment she wandered off to look at them herself.

Nearest lay a long wooden chest, on which were arranged certain contrivances that looked like guns, except that they were short, no more than a foot long; they had triggers and barrels and small curved stocks, so they must be guns! No one had ever seen a gun under four feet long. She looked for the ramrods, but there were none on the chest. Possibly they were cached inside it.

Over the chest in an arch that covered the entire top was a sheet of almost invisible stuff that she touched fearfully. She had never seen anything like it—like frozen water! Hard and cold...She thought of the oiled paper in her father's windows. A sheet of this substance in a window would be a magnificent possession, the envy of every squire in Dolfya. Oiled paper was semi-transparent, while this stuff was like a piece of air.

There was a white square lying beside the tiny guns, with black printing on it. She was deciphering it, painfully, for not only did she read very slowly, even in the priceless old books of her father's library, but this print was in a language slightly different from Orbish, when she felt two hard hands on her waist.

"Get your stinking paws off me," she said, without moving.

She was picked up and set down gently on one side. Revel bent over the chest.

"What are they?"

She thought fast. She had deciphered enough of the card to know they *were* guns: *American handguns of 1940-1975 period*, it said. She couldn't let him know it. The rucker must not get hold of a gun, or he'd attack the gentry themselves, for hadn't he slain innumerable gods already?

"They are children's toys," she said. "I don't know what sort of children would be interested in such weird-looking things."

"Did you ever hear of the Ancient Kingdom?"

She shook her head; the term was new to her.

"The ruck knows of it; the ballad-singers have many sagas of the Ancient Kingdom, but I imagine the gentry have forgotten. It was the world and people of a long time ago. I think these things were walled up here then." His face, really a handsome face if you forgot he was a rucker, screwed up in thought. Then he started to chant something.

"The people of that far-off time,
They carried little guns;
They had so much more freedom
Than we who are their sons."

He stared at the weapons. She thought fast. "These are toy guns, yes. The writing says they are guns for children."

"Maybe the toys of those children worked," he said looking at her.

"You talk nonsense."

He felt the transparent stuff over the chest, pushed on it hard, then raised his pick and struck the stuff a heavy blow.

It shattered into bright daggers and fell on the guns and on the floor. Picking one of the small things from its place, he examined it closely.

"No toy, Lady Nirea," he grunted. "You lied to me."

"I didn't! Can *you* read the writing?" she asked sourly.

"No rucker reads, as you know. But this is no toy, and you knew it." He tucked it into the waistband of his trousers, took three more. "You can show me how to use them later."

She laughed in his face and was given a rough slap on the cheek. Skin tingling, she said, "Play the squire, miner, you don't have long to do it!"

"They won't find this hole."

"I left a trail of emotion that a globe could follow after a week!" she told him.

Slowly his brown face turned pale. Then he struck her again, but very hard, so that she staggered back and fell. Without a word he grasped her wrist and hauled her after him on a swift tour of the cavern.

A huge intricate mechanism sat like a grotesque idol on the floor. "What is it?" he said. "Read for me."

She looked at the printing on the front. *Dynamo* she spelt out, and shrugged. "A name I don't know."

"If you lie to me again, I'll rip that gown off and strangle you with it." He obviously meant it. She said sullenly, "I'm not lying."

"I know you aren't, now. I have an instinct for lies." He dragged her on. "What's this?"

The language was very like Orbish, yet subtly different, and the words were mostly strange. She said aloud, in syllables, *"Man of the 21st century: John R. Klapham, atomic physicist and—"*

"Never mind." He left the big shining case, which was oblong and featureless and seemed made of metal, to pass to something else. Her gaze caught another line on the card as she was pulled away: *Held in suspended animation.* What could the words mean?

They covered the big cave, finding almost nothing they could understand. Here and there were ordinary objects—plates, hides of animals under the near-invisible arches of wondrous material, arrows such as the ruck vagabonds used for shooting birds, candles—but in the main it was a place of mystery.

"The people of the Ancient Kingdom," he said, rubbing his square chin, "put these things into the earth for a purpose. I don't know what it could have been, but I want Jerran to look at them. He's got any number of keen brains."

"Nobody has more than one brain," she snapped.

He grinned. "I have six or eight myself," he said. The creature was totally crazy. He was staring at her again in that lewd way. Now he put a hand on her shoulder. The touch sent hot tingling sensations through her body. The fact that he was of the ruck and no higher than an animal, that he was a god-killer, paled before the desire his great body roused in her. She moved a step toward him, all-but-voluntarily.

His brown eyes lit up. His arm was around her waist, and his lips came near her own. Deep-bred habit made her draw back, but she could not fight the instinct that racked her.

It's a strange place for passion, she thought dazedly; an unknown cavern, full of antique wonders never heard of on earth, filled with a blue haze, and only she and the tall fierce rucker...

CHAPTER FOUR

The Mink has come to the bright sun's light,
His pick is lifted high;
He hears the gentry's whooping yell,
And sees them gallop by.

"Now all too long we've felt the yoke,
And cringed and fawned and died!
'Tis time we turned upon the squire,
To skin his rotten hide!"
　　—Ruck's Ballad of the Mink

Revel was sitting beside the hole in the wall, now filled with rocks, of course; he had replaced the four small guns in his belt and found, by breaking open the chest they'd lain on, a number of boxes of ammunition, with which he'd stuffed his pockets. Experiment had shown him how to load, and tradition of the ruck told him that to shoot, one pointed the end at something (or someone, he told himself grimly) and pulled the small curved projection. The woman should have helped him, but she was sulking in a corner, weeping. She had not wept an hour before!

He wondered if he were the first rucker to hold a gun. Surely the first to have four such tiny weapons, at least.

He heard voices from beyond the wall, filtering in, oddly distorted, through the air spaces between rocks. That was Jerran.

"Yes, he came down here, and threatened me with his pick all dripping yellow, said he'd killed a lot of gods. Crazy, that's what he was!" Jerran's voice broke, a neat bit of acting. "Sure there's an emotion trail! You think I wasn't scared of that maniac? Wasn't he excited? He stayed here a minute and then left again."

That was clever. Jerran had explained away the psychic scent left by the Lady Nirea. He must be talking to a god. But another voice spoke now, and Revel sat up, thinking, The gods don't make sounds!

"Was there a girl with him, a girl of the gentry in a silver gown?"

"No, Lord Ewyo—" it was her father, then— "he was alone."

"He may have hidden her body somewhere," said a heavy voice. Rack, by the Orbs, Revel's brother Rack! "He's turned violent today."

"I understand he's your brother?" said Ewyo.

"Aye. A strong violent man, but worse today than ever."

"No rucker would dare harm Lady Nirea," whined Jerran.

"No rucker should dared have touched her," barked the squire. Then, his voice respectful, he asked, "Can you tell me if she's dead, priest?"

There was a croak like a bull-frog's, a chugarum with words in it. "She lives."

"Where?"

Revel sucked in his breath. If the priest could see all, as they'd been taught, he was doomed. Then, before any other voices beyond the wall could speak, Nirea—he had been a muddleheaded and drooling fool not to seal her mouth—Nirea screamed. "In here, father! Tear down the barricades!"

Revel was on her in two bounds and hit her a crack on the jaw, a vicious blow that sprawled her into a pile of clay tablets (inscribed with writing she had refused to read to him), dead to the world. Then Revel was at the hole, waiting tensely with a gun in his hand.

"What can lie in the rocks?" he heard Jerran say. "The voice was a ghost's."

"Hold your tongue," roared Ewyo. "You'll make a fox for the hunt, small yellow man!"

A gap appeared. "Look in there," said Ewyo, and a head came thrusting in, the head of a squire's servant topped with the distinctive peaked cap and green ear flaps. Revel could not shoot a rucker. He hit the man full in the mouth, and the head disappeared with a howl.

"Tear them down, he's in there. We'll let the zanphs harry him a bit," said Ewyo. "Hear that, rebel?"

"Send in your zanphs," yelled Revel, grinning. "Let 'em come in, squire!"

The gap grew. Up over the rocks charged a zanph, its six legs scrabbling frantically, its snake's head darting back and forth to search him out. He let it see him and utter its war cry, a hiss that became a growl. Then he pointed the gun's muzzle at its face and calmly pulled the curved metal below the barrel. There was a crash as of a mountain falling; dust rained on him from the roof, echoes raged together; and the zanph, its skull fragmented all over four yards of floor, sank to the furred belly and slowly rolled over.

"Send me a globe!" roared Revel, delirious with glee. "Send me a god, Ewyo!"

There was silence beyond the wall; then the priest croaked, "He has a gun. Certainly this is more than a matter of a kidnapped daughter, Ewyo!"

Jerran's voice rose in a laugh. "It is, Lord Ewyo, it is!"

What the hell did the old fellow mean? Revel shrugged. He'd learn later. Now was the time for action.

Going to the prostrate girl, he slung her over his shoulder, a limp light weight. The tattered silver gown flapped as he walked to the hole.

"Stand back," he cried. "I'm bringing your daughter to you, Squire!"

Another zanph showed its horrible reptilian head; he blasted it out of existence with another shot. There were outcries from the squire and his servants, and the priest rumbled, "Sacrilege!"

Rack's head showed between the rocks. "Calm down, boy," he said, his staring walleye gleaming in the lantern light. "You've been living too fast—"

"Not fast enough, Redbeard. Out of the way!"

Rack slowly withdrew, and after kicking a few more boulders from his path, Revel stooped and went out into the tunnel.

"At him!" croaked the priest, a thin man in a radiant blue-green robe, the double scalp lock waving like twin plumes on his shaven head. "Pull him down!"

"Ewyo dies if I'm touched," said Revel coolly, pointing the handgun at the squire's belly.

"Kill him—with that little thing?" said the priest. His voice seemed to come out of the ground, not from such a gaunt frame as his. "You bluff, rucker."

"Look at your zanphs if you think so." He glared at them. There was Ewyo, burly in peach satin and white silk, his long-skirted coat pushed back from a lace shirt, skin-tight pants held by knee-high black boots, a cabbage rose thrust into his cocked hat. There was the priest, lean and savage beneath two hovering globes. Three servants of the squire, Jerran and Rack made up the rest.

"Come here, Jerran," he ordered. Smiling lazily, the little man ambled over. "Take a couple of these miniature guns from my belt. They're loaded. You point them—"

"I can use a gun," said Jerran, "though I never had my hands on one this size."

"They came to us from the Ancient Kingdom," Revel told him.

"Ah," said Jerran, nodding as he pulled two guns from the big man's waistband. "I thought they might have. The ballads say they used such weapons. Everyone carried 'em." He faced the squire, and his small body appeared to swell and toughen as he went on. "Lord Ewyo, please to precede us with your servants and that feather-brained priest. We'll go to the ladders."

Ewyo grunted. Orders from a rucker, to him, *him*, the greatest landholder in Dolfya! But after another glance at the mutilated zanph, he turned and walked down the tunnel.

"Wait a minute," said Revel, but Jerran turned to him with a face as hard and ruthless as a woods lion's. "Shut up, lad," he said. "I'll handle 'em. You just tend to the wench. She's awake, in case you didn't know."

He knew now, for she had just bitten him on the rump. He hoisted her a little higher and absently smacked her buttocks. "Lie quiet, damn you." She lay quiet. He went on marveling at Jerran's commanding new presence, but said nothing. He was behind a born leader now.

Jerran said, "Priest, tell your gods to stop trying to get at my mind. I've shut it off from 'em. You follow Ewyo."

The priest turned on his heel. The servants scuttled after their lord, and Rack sat down on a rock and pulled at his beard, looking thoughtful.

"I don't think it'd be overstating it," he said mildly, "to tell you two you're in trouble."

"So are the gentry, brother," Revel answered.

"That'll be seen. Well," Rack said, squinting his good eye, "I'll be seeing you. Or not, as the case may be."

"Come along," said Jerran, and walked off, followed by Revel with the Lady Nirea.

Ewyo had vanished. His servants, uncertain, were grouped under the ladder, and the priest was mounting up, his radiant robe billowing to show scrawny, hairless legs. The two gods lifted through the murk.

"Ewyo," said Revel, and Jerran interrupted. "Is gone. Did you expect to hold him captive, lad?" He shook his yellow skull. "Too much trouble for two men. Up you go."

Revel sprang at the ladder and was soon crowding the heels of the priest. That worshipful man reached the top of the ladder, turned and knelt and thrust his face into Revel's. It was a vicious face, hawk-nosed and mean. Now it barred his way, gloating openly.

"You're dog-meat, rebel. A shame to kill the Lady Nirea with you, but the gods order it." He reached out a hand and planted it firmly on Revel's face.

Hanging to the rung with his left hand, balancing the girl on the left shoulder, Revel shot up his right and gripped the priest's wrist and heaved up and back, ducking his head at the same time.

The robed man flew into space with a screech.

"Look out below!" roared Revel, and, chuckling, he finished his climb and gave a hand to Jerran. "Where now?" From far below came the crunch of a carcass landing at the foot of the ladders, on the lowest level of the mine shaft. "One less priest!"

"Follow me, lad," said Jerran, and dashed for the entrance. There was no god on duty there, but the two that had accompanied the priest were mounting into the buttoned sky.

The girl was light on his shoulder, a delicious burden, he thought. He hoped he could keep her. Just how, or where, he did not bother to consider. Things were moving too fast for plans, at least plans about women.

Jerran led him up over the crest of the hill above the mine. Beyond lay the uncharted forests of Kamden. He had hunted mink and set rabbit snares on the edges of it since boyhood, but had never seen its depths. So far as he knew, no man had.

As they started toward the wood, the beat of hoofs became audible in the quiet countryside. Revel couldn't see the horses, but he began to run, easily and fast, with Lady Nirea bobbing and swearing on his shoulder. Jerran kept pace.

Then they came up over the rim of the hill behind him, a pack of the gentry on their huge fierce stallions, with a couple of hundred-pound hunting dogs in advance, baying and yapping. The old terrifying viewing call rose: "Va-yoo hallo! Va-yoo hallo allo-allo!" Thousands of the ruck had heard the whooping cry moments before their grisly deaths. Revel tightened his grip on the perfect legs of Nirea, and pounded on. He'd ditch her if need be, but as long as he could hang on to her, by Orbs…

The forest was closer. He could pick out individual trees, oak and silver birch and poplar, standing thick in the matted carpet of thicket and trash. A broad trail opened to the left.

"That way," gasped Jerran, pointing.

"The horses can follow down that road!"

"Don't argue—damn you—lad—just run!"

The gentry came yelling in their wake. A gun banged. Were they shooting at him? Not with the woman slung down his back. The priests might sacrifice a squire's daughter without a murmur, but no gentryman ever harmed a gentrywoman under any circumstances. It was likely a warning. That was why they kept whistling the dogs back, too, for the enormous brutes could rip a human to scarlet rags in twenty seconds, and not even a squire's command stopped them once they'd tasted blood.

He had reached the trees and the wide path. He plunged into it, Jerran beside him; the older man was panting heavily now, but running as strongly as ever. "A little behind me, Revel," he husked out. "See you follow me close."

Jerran knew where he was headed...Revel surrendered all initiative to him. The ground thundered beneath him to the pounding of the horses. He looked back as he ran. They were almost upon him, gay and gaudy in their scarlet, green, fawn and purple hunting clothes; their faces were bloodless, malevolent, and entirely without pity. Several of them carried guns, the long clumsy weapons handed down to them by their grandfathers from the time, a hundred years past, when gun-making was still a known art. Ramrods were fitted below the barrels and the muzzles flared like lilies. He'd back his new-found little guns of the Ancient Kingdom against any such heavy instrument.

Jerran dived into what seemed a solid mass of brambles. Revel shifted the girl and bent to follow; at that instant she grabbed the back of his thigh and wrenched with all her might. He had been carrying her too low again. The tug was just enough to throw him off balance, and rucker and lady sprawled on the forest pathway, entangled together, struggling frantically to rise, as the giant stallions of the gentry bore down upon them.

CHAPTER FIVE

The pretty daughter of the squire,
She came a-riding by;
Of sunlight was her fine long hair,
Of gray flint was her eye.

The Mink he takes her by the arm:
"Now you must come with me!
We'll dwell a space in the wild wild woods
Beneath the great oak tree!"
   —Ruck's Ballad of the Mink

Revel saw the lead horse, a piebald brute with hoofs like mallets, coming at him. The squire atop it was leaning down with the mane whipping his cheeks, smirking at Revel as he drove his steed forward.

He made the fastest decision of his life. He could roll and save himself, for he was quick as a lightning bolt; or he could keep hold of the wench and try to preserve them both.

He could never have told what prompted him to decide to save the Lady Nirea.

At any rate, he threw himself atop her, clamped his arms tight to her sides, and rolled, not toward the brambles, for it was too late for that, but to the center of the path. The piebald crashed by, swerving too late to clip him; the other horses came at him in a solid phalanx. He yanked her up, gaining his own feet by an animal contraction of body. As the heads of the nearest stallions reached him he slipped between them, holding her steady behind him, and praying to the Orbs (from force of lifetime habit) to preserve them for the next minute.

Without Nirea it would have been simple; holding her safe behind him while two lurching horses passed, that made it the trickiest thing he'd ever done. As the squires' legs came abreast, one blink later, he took hold of one of them which was clad in tight blue breeches, and hauled down. Then he leaped forward between the horses' tails, twitching the woman after him with a jerk that almost tore the arm from her body.

The squire in the blue breeches toppled over, howling, and fell on the path. Revel yanked the Lady Nirea to one side as the mass of them swept by, and saw with satisfaction a stallion, trying not to step on the fallen squire, take a nasty tumble itself, flinging its rider ten feet ahead, where he was trampled by a couple of less cautious nags.

Other horses fell over the first one, and the gentry milled about, roaring bloody hell and death on everybody. The two hounds smelled blood and attacked the fallen squires, and Blue Breeches raced off into the woods, one of the ravening dogs at his heels.

Revel made for the other side, the brambles where Jerran had disappeared. He was hauling the girl behind him. A beef-faced squire on a pirouetting horse loosed off his gun at Revel, who snatched a handgun from his belt and fired back. Both of them missed. A gentryman in tan and gold long-skirted coat leaped in front of the miner, the flared muzzle of his gun coming up toward Revel's breast.

Revel shot by instinct, without aiming. The man's face turned into a mess that looked like squashed raspberries. Revel stepped over his body and tried to plunge into the brambles, but he had lost the exact spot, and thorns barred the way.

Then, four feet down the road, Jerran's yellow face popped into view. "Here, lad!"

At that instant Lady Nirea gave a wrench and freed herself from Revel's grip. He whirled and leaped and snatched down, catching the collar of the silver gown. Her momentum carried her forward, but the dress stayed in his hand ripped completely off. He went after her—she was falling now—and caught her, though the atmosphere seemed to be composed equally of gentry and rearing stallions.

Then he turned, carrying her slung over one arm, and managing to reach Jerran's anxious-looking head by knocking down one squire and kicking another in the groin, he dived into the bushes. The Lady Nirea squalled shrilly as the thorns gashed at her soft skin. But Revel blundered on into the bramble patch.

Jerran led him through what seemed impenetrable thickets, following a route that must have been marked, though Revel could not see how. Behind them, the gentry howled and loosed off their guns, but the brambles defeated them, for Revel caught no sounds of pursuit. A scream that thrilled up and choked off must have been the unfortunate Blue Breeches.

Revel looked up, thinking of the globes; he could see the sky in many places through the tangle, but realized that it was probably a thick green solid floor to a watcher from above. A god would have to come very low to see anything moving beneath it.

The woman said bitterly, "For Orbs' sake, at least carry me in some fashion that won't expose *quite* so much of me to the thorns!" She paused and added as an after-thought, "You mudhead!"

He hitched her around and held her curled to his chest, faintly conscious of the smooth body, but concentrating on protecting her from harm; he thought suddenly that he was treating her as if she'd been a ruck woman, instead of one of the gentry, the loathed and feared squirarchy. Was he putting too much importance on the physical attractions that had made him take her?

Jerran was leading him now along a tunnel-like passage of twined, arched shrubbery that made them stoop low. "It'd help if you walked, Lady," he said.

"You may not have noticed it, miner, but I have on just one slipper, and it doesn't have a heel." She scowled up at him. "And when I say one slipper, I mean that's *all*."

"You look fine," he grinned. "No silk and satin looks as attractive as your own pelt, my lady."

They traveled for upwards of half an hour, sometimes down forest lanes that allowed free passage, other times through thickets that ripped their flesh and slowed them to a swearing, sweating crawl. Always there was a screen above them of natural growth, shielding them from the buttoned sky.

At last before them there opened a huge amphitheater of the forest, a hollow with gently sloping sides, covered by a gigantic roof of twined willow wands and twigs. Jerran said, gesturing upward, "That's the biggest piece of camouflage we ever did! The top of it is planted with grass and scrub, rooted in square sods of earth cut from the woods' floor in many places. From above it looks like a round hill rising out of the trees. Took us a year to perfect it."

"Jerran, who is 'us' and—"

"Why, lad, the rebels."

Revel stared at the little man. Could Jerran, the straw-colored stringy fellow he'd worked beside all these years, the quiet one who'd preached serenity and dragged him out of a hundred brawls, could he be a rebel? Fantastic...

The rebels were the anonymous elite of the ruck. They were the malcontents of their society, men whose intellects could not swallow the dreary bromides of the priests, who felt savage indignation against the cruel gentry and the bright, all-mighty globes. It was said that they formed an organization in Dolfya and other cities, these rebels, and that to them could be laid the sabotaging of the coal and diamond mines, the gentry slain in accidents that looked too pat, and the constant aura of uneasy discontent that pervaded the shebeens and all such illegal gathering places of the ruck.

The rebels were highly romantic figures, but Revel had always considered them mythical, for who could think of resisting the condition of Things As They Are? Songs were sung about them over the turf fires, in the squat little huts of the people, and by vagabonds who roamed the countryside by night. The rebels went by fanciful names, as rebels of the people always do; and the one most sung of, most whispered about, in Dolfya at least, was the Mink, who seemed to be a kind of promised savior who would come (soon, always soon) with punishments for the gentry and liberation for the ruck.

So Revel stared at Jerran, mouth agape, and repeated stupidly, "The rebels?"

"Aye, lad! Didn't you ever guess?"

"Orbs, no!"

"Why'd you think I kept stopping your fights in the shebeen?"

"Because you were a pacifist."

The small man shook with laughter. "One, there's nothing I love so much as a good brawl. Two, a brawl might bring the orbs or the gentry to our hidden drink-house, and that'd be bad. Three, a man who's a rebel must appear *not* to be one, even to men he believes he can trust. Four, I've had my eye on you ever since I came from Hakes Town, and didn't want you murdered in a drunken scrimmage. So five, though I hated to do it, I had to preserve you from raging and quarreling until all that brute force and honest fury could be turned to real account for us."

"I can't take it in," Revel said helplessly. "It's as though the heroes of the Ancient Kingdom that we sing about, Rob-'em-Good and Jonenry and Lynka, had met me here. I never believed in rebels, truly, Jerran."

"Why should you? We haven't done anything big yet. We've been searching and waiting for a leader."

Revel snapped his fingers. "The Mink!"

"Yes, the Mink." Jerran looked at him oddly, head cocked like a small yellow bird. "He hasn't come yet, but he will."

Revel looked around him. The amphitheater was dim, lit only by the sunlight that managed to creep in from the forest around it; for no illumination fell from the sodded roof. It must be capable of holding hundreds of men. "How many are you?" he asked.

"Some four thousand and three hundred." There was pride in the man's voice. "After today, Revel, we shall be uncountable thousands. Now the gods have been torn down."

"Not torn down."

"Torn down," repeated Jerran firmly, "from their false 'untouchable' eminence. You've shown the world that the globes can be slain as easily as hares."

"They can still rise into the buttoned sky, and rule from there."

"We'll find ways," grunted Jerran impatiently. "False gods that can die can be lured down by trickery—or we can find a way to go up to the buttons."

"That's insane," said Revel, and would have amplified it, but at that moment the girl spoke.

"When you are quite ready, *Squire* Revel, I wonder if you'd kindly set me down?"

He had forgotten her, slung over his shoulder like a slain doe. Hastily he slipped her off and set her on her feet. She was like a forest nymph, one of those legendary wild women who haunted the trees near towns and lured men to their death; tall and whitely lovely, her stark naked body shone against the greensward with a perfection that made Revel's throat constrict.

Then she doubled up a fist and hit him in the eye.

"You lout!" said the gorgeous creature. "Can't you at least get me something to wear?"

"I can have clothes for you in two minutes, Lady Nirea," said Jerran. "Man's clothes, I'm afraid. No woman has ever seen the meeting place before you."

"Man's clothes—rucker's clothes," she said caustically. "If I'd known what—"

Then her words were muffled by a terrible sound, a noise as of the earth exploding beneath them. Nothing moved, yet they had the sensation of being shaken intolerably by a giant blast of wind. The roar dwindled away, reluctant to cease, and Revel said, "What is it?"

"Come on," said Jerran urgently, "we'll go to the dome and see."

"The dome?"

"The roof of the sanctuary," barked Jerran impatiently. "It holds the weight of a score of men without quivering. We build slowly, but well." He sprinted away.

"The girl!" yelled Revel.

Jerran called over his shoulder, "If she's fool enough to risk woods lions and the bears, let her go!"

Revel stared at Nirea. Then he chuckled. "No gentrywoman could find her way home from this maze-center. You'll wait." He followed his friend.

They shinned up a tree on the edge of the clearing, and jumped to the rim of the dome, which never even swayed beneath their impact. Revel saw it stretch up before him like a grassy hill, and marveled at the rebels' artistry. Shortly they were standing on the crest, and he was clutching at Jerran's arm.

"Orbs above! Look there!"

On the horizon lay a tremendous cloud of gray-black smoke, like the reeking smudge of a forest fire; above it rose another and more ominous cloud, this tinged with red and of mushroom shape.

Revel was speechless, but Jerran ripped out a curse that would have curled the hair of a squire's neck.

"The Globate Credo," he said. "You've proved it wrong in one respect, but there's terrible proof of its truth in another." He spat. "If I figure right, that cloud's hanging over the eastern quarter of Dolfya Town, where none but the ruck lives; and every soul that lived there is dead as last week's dinner."

"The Credo?" said Revel haltingly.

"Sure. Vengeance of the gods comes swift and without warning, below the twin clouds, with a sound of volcanoes. Nobody ever knew what that meant...till now."

CHAPTER SIX

The pretty daughter of the squire,
She mourned and would not eat;
The Mink he tried to tempt her
With barley bread and meat.

"O no, O no, you rebel cur,
I'll never eat nor drink,
Till father's hall I see again!
Till death has trapped the Mink!"
  —Ruck's Ballad of the Mink

There were seven hundred silent men in the amphitheater of the forest, and more came in each minute, slipping from the trees without a sound, taking seats on the sloping grass. Miner's lanterns, the marvelous contraptions that hung in the shafts beside the veins of coal or pockets of diamonds, glowing with a dull penetrating radiance, had been filched from the mines one by one over years, and now illumined the strange hall like blue glowworms spaced around a pit.

Revel sat, uneasy, on the sward in the center, at the bottom of the bowl; beside him were Jerran and Dawvys, the small rebel's cousin who served in the house of Ewyo the squire. There also was the Lady Nirea, dressed in a miner's plain short-sleeved shirt and unornamented pants, but looking as delectable to Revel as she had in the silver gown. She had not spoken to him since the great bang and

124

the twin clouds, but his mind was so full that he didn't care.

He had killed gods. This had brought his whole world down in ruins, shaken his belief in all he had ever been taught by the priests.

He had killed gentrymen, squires whom no breath of trouble from the ruck had ever disturbed. This had made the myths of rebellion very real to him, very possible; and then Jerran had admitted to being a rebel himself.

The east quarter of Dolfya had been wiped out, as Jerran had guessed; men from the town, coming in after dusk, had confirmed it. The place for a square mile was level, featureless, without sign that thousands of people, women and shopkeepers, brewers and doctors, shebeen hosts and small craftsmen and thieves and vegetable-growers, had lived there just this morning. They were all gone into the smoke of the double cloud.

His own mother was dead, then, and perhaps Rack, if the big red man had gone home.

He had taken a squire's daughter and made love to her, love that was returned if only for a brief time; and afterwards he had shot down zanphs with his new-found guns and plummeted a priest to destruction.

So now where was he? Among rebels, certainly, but mentally, where did he stand? Did he espouse the cause of the rebels? He nodded to himself. Of course. Their cause was the ruck's, and Revel was a man of the ruck. He had given the rebels a terrific boost with his god-killing, too. As word went round of it, he could see faces turn toward him, marveling, awe-struck, respectful.

And what was he to do? Become a vagabond, probably, living by night, skulking in the forest edges, passing from town to town hoping he could find a place where the gods had not heard of him, so he might settle down and eventually become a miner again. Mining was all he knew.

He felt for his pick, tucked into his trousers at the back. For all the new handguns, with their ammunition that made hash of a head or a belly, he still preferred his pick. It was the weapon of a man.

He took out a gun from his belt and stared at it. Then he asked Nirea, "What is this called, the curved metal you pull to shoot?"

She glanced over haughtily. "The trigger. Any dolt knows that."

"I wish you'd be nicer. I don't mean to harm you."

"You touched me, and more. I'm dreaming of your torture. Leave me alone."

Jerran stood up. The rebels, who had been buzzing and talking in low tones, quieted until Revel could hear the rabbits hopping in the underbrush beyond the amphitheater.

Jerran began to speak. He told them the whole story of the day, of the gods' death and all. Murmurs and exclamations arose, and he hushed them with a gesture.

"Many of us," he said, "though rebels, have owed allegiance to the gods. Our quarrel has been only with the gentry, whose useless existence and awful power over us are a constant irritation. They who hunt us as 'foxes'— who kill us if we touch them—we have seen are only men like ourselves, women like our women." He pointed to Nirea. "There's a gentrywoman; is she different in body from our wives? Not by so much as a mole!"

"I didn't see any moles," whispered Revel to the girl. She turned red in the face and clamped her teeth together.

"Is her mind different, superior? It's eviller, cruder, more ferocious, maybe, but no whit better than our own! Why then should her kind have power over us?"

The amphitheater roared to the angry yells of rebels. Jerran waved his hand again. "That's been our quarrel with the established way of things in the world. We've hoped for weapons to fight the gentry, and prayed for guidance from the gods. Now we know that the gods are mortal too! They can die! Then they aren't gods, not if gods are the supreme beings we've all been taught! They flee from a miner's pick? Then, by Orbs, they're craven cowards, not fit to be worshipped!"

A hush, then another roar.

"I said we'd waited. The biggest need was a leader, a man of brains and guts and power. We've sung of him for centuries, made up stories of him, songs about him." Jerran paused dramatically. He flung out a finger at the mob. "Who will he be?"

The answer almost broke Revel's eardrums.

The Mink! The Mink! The Mink! The Mink!

"He's here! He's come, from the bowels of the ruck, from the mines, from the people, as he was to come! Already he's done some of the acts the saga-makers put into the Ballad of the Mink!"

Revel frowned. Jerran hadn't told him that the Mink had come at last. The small yellow-faced man went on.

"He's the greatest trapper of mink in Dolfya—his family sleeps under blankets of the little beasts' hides. His own hair is the shade of a mink's pelt, as was foretold. He's as swift and deadly and cunning as the oldest mink alive. He's slain gods and priests, and taken toll of the gentry. I've worked beside him for years, and know his mind and heart have always been ours, though he lived in ignorance of us."

The light, a lurid incredible light, began to dawn on Revel.

Jerran's voice rose to a shriek as the rebels muttered stupefaction. "I tell you I know this is the man we've waited for, us and our fathers and their father's fathers before them! Rebels of Dolfya, I show you—*Revel, the Mink!*"

The shouts that had come before were murmurs to the chorus of stentorian bellows which assaulted Revel's ears now. The woman turned and said something to him, her fine face disdainful, but the words were lost in the tumult. A dozen men surged down and lifted him to their shoulders and paraded him round, while hands reached up to touch him and wave greeting to him.

It was the beginning of a celebration he had never seen the like of, a festival occasion that included a great dinner of boar and deer meat and stolen gentry's wine, over which much vague planning was done; and it ended only when the last rebel had left to sneak homeward, and he and the girl were left alone with Jerran.

"Sleep now, lad," Jerran said, grinning. "You're exhausted. It isn't every day a man finds himself a savior."

"But the Mink—I, the Mink?" He still had not entirely accepted it.

"I think so…and if I care to call you the Mink, no one can contradict me."

"All the while I was doing those things this morning," muttered Revel, "I had the feeling I'd done them before. I must have been remembering the old ballad, for by Orbs, the acts do fit!"

"That minor blasphemy begins to annoy me," said Jerran seriously. "It's like saying 'by the man I killed yesterday.' We've got to revise our swearing habits."

"Why not substitute *Revel* or *Mink* for *Orb?*" asked the girl harshly. "Our Revel who dwells in the buttoned sky," she added, with a malevolent sneer.

"Ah, go to sleep, both of you," said Jerran. "Tomorrow we start to plan—really plan—to overthrow the gentry."

"And the priests," said Revel fiercely, "and the gods!" He almost believed that somehow they could climb into the air and destroy the gods in their red and blue buttons. He lay down, one hand vised on the woman's wrist, and though he felt he should never sleep that night, being far too excited, in three minutes he was snoring mightily.

He woke some time later with the prickling feeling of danger on his skin. He opened his eyes and saw red, literally a red mist that obscured the world. Then his head began to open and shut, open and shut, and he knew he had been hit a hell of a blow on the forehead, and there was blood in his eyes.

Groping for his pick, that had lain next his left hand, he missed it; then he recalled the girl, reached out for her, found she was gone too. He drew the back of his arm over his eyes and cleared the gore a trifle. "Jerran?" he said quietly. No answer.

Blinking, he saw the vast meeting place empty, lit by the blue lanterns. He rolled his head and there, its point buried deep in the sward an inch from his right ear, was his pick. He sat up. Jerran lay a dozen feet off, looking very dead indeed, with his thin hair matted with blackening blood.

Instinctively he tore the pick out of the ground. It was buried so deep that only a very strong hand could have sent it in; not the girl, he thought, somehow relieved that she hadn't done it. No, a miner's blow alone might have done it, for the earth was packed solid as oak's wood by untold multitudes of rebels' feet.

Wait a minute, he said to himself: this is all wrong. That blow should have opened my skull like a walnut. It missed me by a fraction—either the aim was poor, or else damned good. I could have struck such a blow, sure to miss where I wished to, but not even many miners could duplicate it.

Had the enemy missed, then walloped him with another weapon and left him for dead? Gingerly he felt the wound on his head. It was healing already, a tap that might have laid him out for a few hours, but would never have slain him.

He glared at the pick in his hand. Then he brought it up and in the combined light of the blue lanterns and the dawn filtering in from the woods, he squinted at the handle.

Where his own pick bore the crude carving of a mink (he had taken the beast as his symbol a long time ago, another sign of his identity), this one had a jumble of grooves meant to represent a woods lion.

This wasn't Revel's pick—it was his brother Rack's!

Caught in an appalling dream that was the hardest reality he'd ever faced, he pored over the pickax, scanned the motionless form of his friend Jerran, then goggled foolishly at nothing in particular as he thought of his situation, stranded in a place he could not escape from alone, with many half-formed plots in his head but no way to carry them out. Between him and Dolfya, and the other rebels, lay miles of tangled forest no man, be he ever so skillful at woodscraft, could penetrate without the knowledge of a route; thousands of the ruck were depending on him to lead them, and he couldn't even lead himself home.

"If you're the Mink, Revel m'lad," he said aloud, "it's time you came up with a brilliant idea!"

And there wasn't a scheme in his head.

CHAPTER SEVEN

The haughty maid has left the Mink,
She finds her father's place;
The squire has looked her in the eye:
"Now what a fox to chase!"

He's called in all his friends and kin,
And dealt out guns and shells;
He's sworn an oath to catch the Mink
By all the seven hells!
—Ruck's Ballad of the Mink

Lady Nirea was puffing and blowing and clawing her way through endless miles of creepers, thorns, and brushwood. She wished Revel were carrying her now, even if it meant the loss of her clothing again. Now she appreciated what a job he'd done, for naked though she'd been, not half as many scratches had marred her skin on their first journey.

Ahead of her, the giant called Rack was doing his best to break trail for her; and in front of him, with a rope under his arms which the red-bearded man held tightly, went Dawvys, her father's servant.

As she understood the tale from Rack's few sentences, growled out in a voice that reeked with hatred of somebody, whether herself or Revel or whom she couldn't tell, he had caught Dawvys just emerging from the forest and made him lead the way back to the domed glade. Ewyo the squire had sent Rack out for her, and Rack was evidently all a rucker should be—faithful, reverent, and obedient to the least command of the gentry.

She remembered waking, Revel's strong hand still clamped on her wrist, and seeing this walleyed brute just aiming a swing of a pick at his brother's head. She had screamed, and Rack had missed. She wondered whether he had meant to hit at all. There was already a bloody gash on Revel's scalp, and the little yellow man, Jerran, lay quite still with red trickling out of his head.

Then Rack had picked up Revel's pick and disengaged the grip of his hand (was it as cold and lifeless as she'd thought? could the Mink be dead?) from her wrist, and booted Dawvys out on the trail.

That had been hours ago. They were still bumbling through the forest, although the sun was high.

"He's leading us wrong," she panted. "Don't trust him. He's an important rebel."

"He wants to live as badly as we do, Lady. He'll take us home."

And sure enough, they had come shortly to the rim of the woodland. She swayed and nearly collapsed. "Give me your arm, rucker," she said. "I give you permission to touch me."

His arm was like stone, supporting her along the road to Dolfya's outskirts where her father's mansion lay. After a few minutes he dropped the rope that held Dawvys. "Damn," he said loudly, "he will get away!" and bent to retrieve it. Dawvys leaped off like a pinched frog, and Rack said grimly, "No use to chase that one, he can sprint faster than a dozen hulks like me."

"You let him go," said Nirea.

He turned his blue eye on her. "That is as you see fit to believe, Lady."

She would turn him over to her father's huntsman, she thought. Or would she? He'd saved her...was this gratitude in her mind? It was a foreign emotion. Wait and see, she told herself; don't fret now. She was very tired.

They came to the house of Ewyo, a sprawling erection of field stone and ancient brick dug from distant ruins of another time. No one could make bricks like that now. She touched the gate in the wall and instantly a dozen hounds, gaunt and savage, came leaping from the lawns. Recognizing her, they fawned, and she opened the gate. "Come in," she said. He grunted and obeyed, eyeing the dogs.

In the library of the house, which contained more than twenty priceless books allowed her ancestors by the gods, she met her father, the squire Ewyo. He scowled up at Rack.

"You bring this rucker, this miner, into the library, Nirea?"

Not a word of greeting, she thought, not a single expression of relief at her safety. For the first time she began to contrast the manners of the gentry with those of Revel. He was rough, true, and crude and inclined to glory in his animal strength, and he had made love to her, to boot; but if he had found her after thinking her dead, by the Orbs! he wouldn't have snarled out something about an unimportant convention!

"The man saved me at great risk, and killed his own brother doing it," she said coldly. She would not mention Dawvys at all. Not now! "He deserves a reward, Ewyo, and not harsh words from you."

He slapped his high sleek boots with a hunting crop. He was a burly, beefy-looking man, nothing like the lean tough Mink. She felt a sense of revulsion. She turned to Rack and stared at the big face, scarred by whipping branches, firm and fearless, as hard as the heart of a mountain. "Go home and get some sleep, Rack," she said kindly. "You'll hear from me later."

"I have no home, Lady," he answered. "The gods destroyed our part of the town yesterday."

Ewyo snorted, "Dawvys can give him a bed for now in the servants' huts. Dawvys!"

It was on her tongue to say that Dawvys wouldn't be likely to answer his bawl, but the man appeared in the doorway, spruce and clean, with only a few scratches to tell of his activities. "Yes, Lord Ewyo?"

"Take this rucker and find a bed for him. Jump!"

"Yessir." Dawvys, a plump fellow with no hint of his enormous endurance in his look, motioned Rack out of the library.

Ewyo said, "Well! How are you, Nirea? Your sister Jann and I have been worrying."

"I'm all right."

"Did you suffer indignities at the hands of that crazy miner?"

He looked like a damned red-faced bear, she thought, and surprised herself by saying, "Revel treated me with— with much consideration."

"Huh! Wouldn't have thought it. You want to sleep?"

"Don't bother about me," she said, turning. "Get on with your pressing business, father." She went to her room and lay down on the satin-sheeted bed without even removing the tattered rucker's clothes. For a long while she lay there, thinking. Then she did a thing that no one could ever have convinced her she'd do till that day. She changed into a sheer black gown, after bathing of course, and slipped downstairs to her father's private room.

She had never been in it, no one but Ewyo had; she had no clear notion of what she was looking for. But an army of questions warred in her mind, and it seemed to her that there were secrets she must discover: answers which she had never looked for, explanations for things she had always taken for granted.

For instance, she thought, turning the handle slowly and without noise, why were the gentry the gentry? Why did the gods allow almost anything to her kind, when the ruck had no rights? She shook her head. All her breeding said she was mad, yet she opened the door of the private room and walked in.

Dawvys whirled from where he had been bending over a huge leather-bound book on a table. His face was white, but it cleared of panic when he saw her.

"The Lady Nirea moves silently."

"What are you doing here?" she asked sharply.

"The same thing you mean to do, Lady. I'm seeking the answers to certain problems."

"Can a rucker read minds like a globe?"

He laughed. "It was an obvious guess, Lady."

"And have you found answers, Dawvys?"

He sighed. "I cannot read, as the Lady knows. No rucker reads."

She watched his face a moment. "Stay here," she said. "*I* can read."

"The Lady of the Mink is kind," he said, bowing. The title did not shock her. Strangeness on strangeness!

The book was full of queer writing, like none she had ever seen. Instead of letters that each stood alone, the letters were joined, each word being a unit without a break; and they seemed to stand up a little from the page, not being sunken into the paper as all printing was that she had seen.

With difficulty she read a few sentences.

"This day the third in the month of Orbuary I did feed the gods, more than forty of them in the morning and twenty after eating. I am so weak I can hardly hold this pen."

"What does it mean?" asked Dawvys.

"I don't know." She flipped a page. "This day did hunt the fox, he being a strong untiring trapper who was found with forbidden ale cached in his house, and chased him over eight mile before he went to earth in a spinney, where the dogs found him and tore him to bits. Afterwards did feed nine gods, who have drained me so I cannot see but in a fog," she read aloud.

"That's your father speaking," whispered Dawvys, "He hunted a trapper last month."

"But how is it down here, if it was Ewyo? The books were made many years before my grandfather was born. No one makes books now. The art is lost."

"Nevertheless, I think Ewyo made this one himself. Unless it's a prophecy of the gods." He turned the book over. "What does it say on the outside?"

She read it with cold grue inching up her back. "Ewyo of Dolfya, His Ledger and Record Book."

"Then he did make it."

"How? How could he? The art is lost!"

"Many things the ruck believed have been proved false in these last hours," Dawvys said. "Perhaps the gentry's beliefs are equally wrong."

She left the book and went to a desk by the oiled-paper window. A drawer was partly open. Inside was a big heap of dandelions, thick grasses, and wild parsley. She remembered Jerran's taunt, "Your father eats dandelions!"

"Dawvys, why are these here?"

"I don't know, Lady. I gather them and the squire eats them, but why, I can't say."

There was a sound at the door. Dawvys sprang toward the brocaded hangings, too late; Ewyo thrust in his head, black rage on his features.

"What in the seven hells are you doing here, Nirea?"

The habits of a lifetime couldn't be overcome by a day in the presence of the Mink. She said quickly, "I saw Dawvys come in, father, and followed him."

"Oh. Good for you. Dawvys, report yourself to the huntsman for a fox!"

Dawvys bowed and went out. She breathed freely; he would escape, and still she'd saved herself. What Ewyo might have done to her, she didn't know, but she feared him when he was roused.

She yearned to ask him about the book and the weeds, but didn't dare. She passed him and went to the resting room, where she occupied a chair for an hour, blankly pondering the tottering of her universe.

At last she stood up. She was a gentrywoman, she had guts in her belly. Why shouldn't she ask her father questions? Before she could think about it and grow scared, she went searching, and ran across her sister Jann.

Jann was twenty-four, a tall ash-blonde woman with snaky amber eyes and pointed ears who lorded it over the household.

"Have you seen Ewyo?"

"He's in the private room."

She headed for it, and Jann ran to catch at her arm. "You can't disturb him there!"

"I've been in it before."

Jann clawed at her. "You haven't! Even I was only there once…"

"Even you. My, my." Nirea walked on, Jann tugging at her futilely. "I have to talk to him."

"Stop! Damn you, you whelp, you can't—"

With precision and force, Nirea socked her sister in the left eye. Then she strode down the hall and knocked on the door of the private room and immediately went in.

The sight that greeted her, completely incomprehensible, was still as revolting and horrifying a thing as she had ever seen. Her father lay back in a big armchair, relaxed and half-asleep to judge from his hanging arms and barely open eyes. A curious sound, a kind of brrm-brrm, came from his chest.

Resting on his throat was a golden globe. Two of its tentacles were pushed almost out of sight into his nostrils, two more dipped into his gaping mouth. The remaining four waved slowly above the squire's face.

Nirea screamed.

The globe floated upward, slowly, grudgingly. Its tentacles withdrew from the squire. Ewyo stirred and opened his pale eyes to glare at her. A flush of hideous fury spread up his cheeks. He struggled to his feet and lurched over and slapped her face, so that she ceased to scream and fell against the wall, moaning. The squire stood over her.

"You meddlesome bitch, I ought to have you cut up for the hounds!"

"In the name of the Orbs," she said, whimpering, "what were you doing?"

He grimaced at her like a madman. "You're not supposed to be told till you're twenty, and you don't do it yourself till you reach twenty-eight."

"*Do it myself.*"

"Certainly." He gave a humorless snort of laughter. "D'you think we don't pay for the privilege of being gentry, you fool? Now leave me alone!" He lifted her and flung her at the door. The golden sphere hovered motionless in the air. "Never speak of what you saw, and never ask another question of me till your twentieth birthday…if you live to reach it!"

She fumbled the door open and staggered into the hall, and wept there with awful tearing sobs, while her sister Jann looked at her and giggled hysterically.

CHAPTER EIGHT

The Mink he seeks the gentrylass;
He eyes the gods above;
He laughs their might to scorn, the while
He hunts his highborn love.

A fearsome lion bars the way,
The Mink he cannot pass;
He lifts his pick with fearful rage,
And blood besmears the grass!
　　—Ruck's Ballad of the Mink

Revel was plowing through the brush like a wound-crazed bear. Jerran came behind, shouting directions, for Revel's impatience would not be stilled enough for him to follow anyone, especially the small Jerran, whose head rang, he said, from the skull-cracking blow he'd been given by Rack, and who was slowed as a consequence.

Revel got farther and farther in advance, tearing with his pick at vines and creepers, trampling small trees, making enough noise for seven men. Dimly he remembered much of the trail hereabouts, and at last he was so far ahead of Jerran that he couldn't hear him.

He came into a tiny glade, ceilinged with branches of the oaks. Across its width, some twenty feet from him, a huge woods lion lay above the torn corpse of a man. One of the rebels from the meeting, thought Revel, who wasn't so lucky as most. The lion looked up and growled.

Its mane was long and bur-tangled, black as sin; its body seven hundred pounds of muscle and bone, was longer than Revel was tall. He greeted it joyously, a foe to grapple with at last!

It came to its feet, challenge on challenge rumbling in its massive chest. He drew a gun, then stuck it back. His hands ached for work, more work than the pulling of a trigger. He ported his pickax. "Come along, old monster," he said. "We'll see how a mink and a lion can mix it!"

It stalked two steps, gathered itself for a leap; he didn't wait, but sprang forward to meet it. The lion rose, checking its pounce with surprise, for surely no man had ever charged *it* before. The pick swung down as it struck sideways at Revel, catching it in one shoulder, tearing the flesh like dough. It screeched, clawing for him.

One of the scimitar claws caught his side, gashing shirt and skin. Revel whirled, yelling, flung himself on the animal's back, grabbed a handful of mane with his left hand, and buried the pick in the center of the woods lion's skull. The carcass lost its stiffness, sagged and fell, leg bones cracking like gun shots as the tremendous body came down upon them. Revel sprang to one side, lighting on his feet.

"Not bad," said Jerran drily, coming into the glade. "If you're quite through, Revel, we might be going along?"

"I had to find out if I'm really the Mink," explained Revel, retrieving his pick from the splintered bone of the lion's head. "The Mink could slay a woods lion with one blow, it says in the ballads. This fellow took me two blows."

Jerran said, his face twisted, "Damn you, don't get cocky on me! You're important now, no dirty miner, but a leader! If you haven't got the brains to lead, at least keep still, follow my orders, and be a figurehead. But don't take chances for the fun of it, because your lousy hulk may be the salvation of man, despite yourself!"

Revel hung his head. Jerran looked at him a moment. "Nerves, that's it, and excitement, and eagerness to do something with your big hands. You're young, and I shouldn't expect strict attention to duty of you. But I *do*, blast it! Now march!"

When they had traversed the forest, they emerged a little west of Dolfya, on a stretch of dirt road bordered by maples. The lane seemed deserted. Here and there in the buttoned sky were the bright dots of gods passing back and forth between their abodes. Jerran led him purposefully down the road.

Suddenly a man came bursting out from the maples and ran headlong into them, knocking the small man back into Revel's arms. It was Dawvys, clothing disheveled, mouth agape with running. "They are after me!" he panted. "Ewyo sentenced me to the hounds. I ran, but they're after me!"

Revel hauled out his pick. "Look there," he said, jerking his head upward. "Concentration of orbs above us."

"They point the way for the squires," grunted Jerran. "I don't hear the dogs, though."

"Ewyo wants me alive."

"He won't get you!"

"Will I not?" Ewyo himself had stepped quietly out from the trees, directly in their path. In puce velvet, a great trumpet-mouthed gun in his hands, he stood beefy and menacing before them. "Do you tell me I won't, Revel the Mink?" He chuckled icily at the looks of amazement. "D'you think I wouldn't have rucker spies? D'you think we don't know about your foolish hideaway in the forest, and couldn't clap our hands down on all of you in an hour if we wished to?" Two more squires, tall and red-faced and prominently armed, came out behind him. "Gentles," said Ewyo with mock politeness, "I give you Revel, the Mink, and two minor henchmen."

Revel lifted his pick and came forward, roaring defiance. Ewyo's gun thrust out at his belly. "Don't die now," said the big squire pleadingly. "I want you for a fox, Revel."

Jerran snatched a handgun from his belt. One of the squires loosed off at him instantly, the slug striking the handgun more by accident than design, sending it spinning as Jerran howled and gripped his numbed fingers.

"Nice shooting, Rosk," said Ewyo. Revel still stood with his pick raised, wondering what his chances of a swipe at Ewyo would be. "Put it down," said the squire. "Drop it!"

"Drop it, Revel," said Jerran. The Mink did so, and Rosk picked it up.

"Come along," said Ewyo then. "I have some excellent torture rooms I'd like you to inspect. Personally!" With a grin like a weasel's, he motioned them through the maples. Several others of the gentry came up, and the three rebels were surrounded and marched off to the great house of Ewyo of Dolfya.

The room was large, of field stone, set below the house like a mole's den; portions of the walls were black with age-old soot, from what hellish fires Revel did not like to guess, and the rafters were grimed and looked like axe-blades, darkened with dry blood, ready to fall upon him. One wall had thongs hanging from it, beside a nine-lashed whip hanging on a post. Candles illumined other instruments, the purpose of all of which was torture.

"Strap him to the wall," said Ewyo. Two of his servants did so; they were evil-faced ruckers, fat with good living in the squire's huts. Rosk, the lean-jawed, red-cheeked squire who was Ewyo's closest friend, said, "Shall I flay a part of him? The left hand, say, or one foot so he'll be slow in the hunt?"

"No. I want him hale and hearty." Revel breathed easier. "The gods want to do something, though. I'm not sure what. I have my orders." Ewyo took a seat by the wall, gestured his servants out. As the door closed behind them, a hideous yell echoed in the vault.

Ewyo said comfortably, "They are taking the hide off the back of Dawvys, in the next chamber. They'll split his fingernails, too, and perhaps take off an ear. He's the least important of you upstarts, and I don't care if he's as slow as a slug tomorrow."

Revel thrashed impotently in the leather straps.

Rosk studied the face of the Mink. He opened his gash of a mouth to say something, and Revel spat accurately into it. "I wish it were my pick," he said, as the squire sputtered and backed off.

"Let be, Rosk," said Ewyo, smiling a little. "He'll pay for it tomorrow." Rosk wiped his lips as the burly squire cocked his head, listening to an unseen command. Then he walked over, opened the door, and let in another yelp of agony, followed by a pair of golden orbs, with their attendant zanphs.

The globes floated down to the level of the Mink's face, and his skin prickled at the nearness of the energy aura. What now? The long feelers came darting out, touching his eyelids, his cheeks, and Revel winced, expecting a searing burn. There was only the tingle. They could regulate the energy, then, burning an opponent only when necessary. But how loathsome their nearness was, to a sane and enlightened man who had discarded the creed of their god-hood!

Now their minds came probing into his. Automatically he erected the rampart of innocuous thoughts. Yet the probing continued; he could feel it as a tangible finger of force, needling here, thrusting in there, pressing aside the thoughts that meant nothing, feeling out not only his true thoughts, but his memories, his unconscious hopes, the very traits of character which made him what he was and of which he was scarcely aware.

This was no casually suspicious probing, such as an orb might give a man as it passed him in the mine. This was a brutal wrenching of brain-stuff that would not be denied. He felt it go into his rebellious brain, poke and pry, ferret out all he remembered and believed. All the conceit washed out of Revel the Mink. All the scorn he had felt for these creatures turned to fear, and the bitter hatred increased a thousandfold. And he knew that they felt it as it happened.

At last the feelers drew back, and the orbs lifted toward the rafters. Their zanphs lay watching them, and the two squires stood up uncertainly. Then Rosk said in a hollow, unreal voice, "This man is to be guarded closely. He must not be allowed to escape. It would be better if he were killed now, rather than kept for the hunt. He is the most dangerous rebel we have ever found."

The Mink realized that the gods were using Rosk as a dummy, speaking through his lips.

Ewyo said, looking at the globes, that burnt with a dull radiance in the upper gloom, "It would be better if he were hunted down. He is the 'Savior' the ruck has been waiting for all these years, they think, and if we slew him in this chamber, his death would never be believed. He should be hunted before the whole town, and torn to pieces by the dogs."

The globes, through Rosk's lips, said, "That is so. Hunt him, then; but if he escapes, you die and your family's status is reduced to that of the lowest rucker's." They floated toward the door, which Ewyo hastened to open for them. The sound of Dawvys' groans came in, and Revel strained again at his bonds.

Ewyo's pale eyes darted toward him. "What a fox you'll make," he gloated. "We'll run you in my own lands, which are the best for the game in all this country. We'll run you naked, I think, and allow the ruck to gather on the hills and watch you scuttle from afar. Their precious savior! A naked, frightened, harried rabbit, instead of a bold fighting mink! How'll they like *that*? How much talk of treason will there be for the next ten years, after *that*? Precious little, Revel of the Ruck!"

He called his servants. "Take him and bind him with two dozen thick thongs, and have twenty men sit in a circle

round him all night. Give him plenty of food and water—
by Orbs, give him a beaker of my wine! We'll have a fox
tomorrow to remember for a lifetime!"

CHAPTER NINE

And now the squire has trapped the Mink,
And now he sets him free,
And now the Mink is hunted down
On hill and vale and lea.

He pants and gasps, his legs grow weak,
His eyes with sweat are blind;
In squire's halloo and hound's mad bark
He hears his death behind!
    —Ruck's Ballad of the Mind

They took Revel to the top of a hill just behind Ewyo's
mansion. He was stripped to the buff, but on his feet were
stout sandals of horsehide in triple thickness, so that he
could run well and give them a good hunt. On the crest
they untied him, and he stood naked in a ring of the horsed
gentry, rubbing his wrists and glaring at them. Beside him
were Jerran and the mutilated Dawvys, who both wore
their customary shirts and trousers.

Running his eyes over the squirachy, Revel saw with a
strange thrill of horror the Lady Nirea, on a deep-chested
roan stallion, as cool and distant as the moon...and as
beautiful, he thought bitterly. Well, but hadn't he had her?
He, a rucker born had loved this woman of the gentry! Let
her watch him die—small compensation that would be!

He bowed to her. "May you be in at the death," he said
clearly, and had the satisfaction of seeing her face go white.

"Give the Mink his fangs," said Ewyo. The burly squire was all in scarlet silk and purple velvet, with white calfskin boots on his thick legs. At his command, Rosk threw the tall rebel a belt with two holsters, in which were thrust two short iron daggers. "By rights you should go without, Mink," said Ewyo, "but it's more sport to chivvy a fox with a bite in him. Now, you have till the count of three hundred."

"Five hundred is customary," interrupted Nirea.

"Three is plenty for the savior of the ruck. Hold your tongue, Lady." He leaned over his steed's head. "Three hundred, Mink, and then we come after you. Your course is down this hill and straight away toward the sea. Don't try to escape the straight, either, because the hills are rimmed with guards who'll blow your guts out if you cross the line; and some thousands of your slimy kin are clustered on those hills to watch their hero die." He nodded to the woman beside him, a blonde wench with vicious amber eyes. "Begin the count, Jann."

The blonde said loudly, "One, two, three—" and at the third word Revel was off, running like a slim brown stag down the slope of the hill. Behind him came Dawvys and Jerran. The little man cried, "Don't wait, Revel lad. Save yourself if you can. Remember you're the Mink!"

"I wish to Orbs I wasn't," he growled, and hit the bottom, skimmed over a patch of raw rocks and struck the green beyond. As he ran he buckled the belt around his waist, with a knife hanging on each hip. He had not expected these, and though Ewyo thought he'd lose only a hound or two, Revel intended to take at least a pair of squires with him into the unknown...

He was a fine runner. By the time Lady Jann had counted two hundred and fifty, he was half a mile down the straight, which was a belt of land some quarter of a mile wide and twenty long, ending above the sea on a cliff's edge. As the squire had said, he would not be able to break off the straight, for guards and packed mobs lined it and a naked man would be far too conspicuous heading toward them.

Now he thought of his two comrades in ill fortune. Neither of them was a runner of any caliber. Should he wait and help them?

Selfishness said *no*—and unselfishness said *no*, for wasn't his first duty to the ruck, not to his friends? Didn't he owe it to humanity to save himself? And besides, he was a lusty young buck, and didn't want to die.

But he glanced back, slowed, waited till the two had come panting up to him, and thrusting an arm around each waist, ran them forward with him, ignoring their protests.

They came to a coppice of elms, grown thick with brambles and cluttered with deadwood. It covered perhaps an acre. Revel ploughed into it, cursing as the thorns stabbed his naked hide. Too late he realized he should have skirted it. In the rare quarter-seconds when the branches were not snapping or the brush whipping noisily aside from their progress, he could hear the faint barking of the great hounds; even, he thought, the whoops of the excited gentry as they started down the hill on their fiery stallions. He pictured Nirea, her slate-hued eyes gleaming, her creamy skin aflush as she leaned forward eagerly for the first sight of the Mink. Damn her!

Abruptly the earth slanted off to the right, so that Revel, who was still pushing Dawvys and Jerran, went headlong into a patch of nettles, losing his balance at the unexpected dip and shoving both companions down on their faces. Dawvys rolled, yelping at the pain of scratches on fresh wounds, then vanished with a howl. Revel crouched, staring, unbelieving. In a moment the head of the plump rucker came up out of the earth.

"What in Orbs' names—"

"It's a pit," said Dawvys. "It was covered with trash." His eyes were wide and frightened. "Go on, Revel. I can't run another step."

The Mink thought swiftly. Dawvys was right, he could run no longer. Quickly Revel shoved the man's head down, threw several branches and bushes across the mouth of the pit, began to disguise it, talking as he worked.

"Lie down and be very still, old fellow. Jerran and I will make enough of a trail for the hounds to follow, and only bad luck will discover you to them. If we escape, we'll come back tonight for you." The pit was camouflaged, looked like a mound of trash beside the trail. Revel murmured a good-bye, and went plunging on through the coppice to the other side, Jerran following him nimbly with the strength of second wind.

Now they could truly run, for Jerran, though forty-two, was no antique; and Revel had the thews of a woods lion. The way before them was smooth, grass cropped close by the sheep of Ewyo, gently rolling mounds one after another so that skimming down one slope gave them impetus to dash up the next. A faint cheer came to them from the left. The ruck was on their side.

Perhaps if I die well enough, thought Revel, my death may spark a revolt, and so count for something. He felt at the hilt of the iron daggers. Just give me Ewyo, he prayed to whatever higher powers there might be; just let me have one thrust at Ewyo the Squire!

From the crest of the highest hill he looked back, as Jerran sucked for breath. The gentry were just topping a rise some half mile behind. Not bad! But the dogs were much closer. They had gone through the coppice without discovering Dawvys; now, with any luck, they never would.

Revel ran on. His feet thudded on rock, slithered on grass, shuffled through the mire of a narrow swampland. Here trees slashed at him, there a woodchuck sprang out of his path and made him stumble with sudden panic. His chest labored, drawing in air; his legs pumped and ached. Then he came to a river.

It was some ten yards broad, with a swift current. He said to Jerran, "If we can make headway against that current, land up-stream on the other side, we may have a chance."

The runty yellow man shook his head. "Look up," he gasped. Above them soared a score of globes, plainly marking their position for the gentry.

"The filthy schemers," growled Revel. "The foul cheats! They call this a game, yet 'tis as easy for them as it would be to shoot at us in a small sealed room!" He bent down. "Get on my back, little one." Jerran climbed on, and Revel grasped his legs, told him to hang tight around his neck, and leaped into the river.

Only thirty feet across, it was yet quite deep, and Revel sank like a dropped rock. When the water above his head was so opaque that he could not distinguish anything save a dull mirky lightness, he struck out downstream. For a full minute he swam with the current, then began to rise, Jerran clinging weakly to his neck. The Mink thanked his Orbs—no, not them, but whatever brought him luck—that he was one of the few ruckers who had taught himself to swim...

He had gone farther by swimming than he might have running, for the current was like a demon with a thousand legs, all speeding it on and carrying him with it. His head lifted clear of the waters in the center of the stream, and Jerran behind him broke into coughs and gurgles. Revel looked for globes, and saw them upriver, lifting and falling uncertainly. He said, "Take a breath!" did so himself, and sank again. This time he stayed under for the space he could have counted fifty, then rose again near the far bank.

He was among trees, birch and poplar and evergreen, that grew to the water's brink. He struggled ashore, carrying a limp Jerran, and fell with his burden beneath a single giant oak, which sheltered him from the buttoned, all-seeing sky.

"Rest a while, Jerran. We've put plenty of distance behind us."

Yet when he stood up and gave his friend a hand, five minutes later, he could already hear the baying of hounds.

A touch of panic threaded down his spine—not the panic that flared and died when a woodchuck startled him, but the panic of any hunted creature who, do what he may, still hears the pursuers close behind him. The sound of the howls told him the dogs had crossed the river. He looked up, but saw no orbs. No dog scents a man two miles off. Who had betrayed them? Or were the gentry presuming that they must have crossed?

He broke trail for Jerran through a section that a great bear would have found hard going, all vines and tough saplings and snake holes that sunk beneath his sandaled feet. His body was by this time a hatched network of pain and scarlet stripes, oozing blood.

He had expected the mass of impeding vegetation to be a thin patch at best, but it went on and on, and the trees thinned so that the sky was open above them. It was a matter of time only till the globes spotted him. The hounds were louder. Once he heard the shout of a man, thin and high in the distance.

At last he was on solid, uncluttered ground again. He looked down at his skin, wondering if it would ever be smooth and whole again. His body had been gouged, gashed, torn, disfigured.

"Va-yoo hallo! Va-yoo hallo-lo-lo-lo-lo!" The terrible cry rang behind him, and turning, he saw two horsemen cresting a hill to the side of the patch of bad ground.

Then it dawned on him how they had been followed; for behind the stallioned squires rose the hills, which bordered the straight hunting course, and on them showed small dots of color, the keen-eyed watchers of the gentry. No matter where he ran on this long narrow coursing ground, there would be eyes upon him.

At least the ravening dogs were not nearby. He picked up Jerran, tucked him under one arm, and dashed for the shelter of the evergreen woods before him. The hoofs of the horses pounded behind. He dodged in among the pines, and the mournful call lifted— "Gone to earth! Go-ho-hon to earth!"

"Damn you, put me down!" rasped Jerran. "Am I a child, to be carted like this?" Revel dropped him. They skittered from tree to tree, and then a charging horse was on them, and Jerran was rolling aside, bleating with fear of the hoofs, while Revel turned and stood foursquare in the path. As the stallion all but touched him, he jumped aside, jumped back, so that the head of the beast passed him but the rider was struck and clutched and hurled from his saddle, losing his trumpet-gun as he fell. The Mink was sitting astride him before he could bounce up, and two ruthless hands took him by the throat and tore out his jugular. The second rider at that instant drew rein behind them, and lifted his own gun for a quick shot.

Jerran hurled a rock. It took the squire on the head, spilled him out of his saddle, and the subsequent proceedings interested him no more.

"Two guns, by Orbs!" crowed Revel, gathering them up. "And two horses!" He put a foot into the stirrup of the second one, but it shied madly at the touch of a bloody, naked man; dashed forward, startling the other, and together they vanished among the trees. "Hell!" said Jerran, taking one of the guns; "nothing gained but two bullets, Mink."

"Two bullets is two more slain squires. Come on!"

The evergreens gave out shortly, and they were in a valley channeled by sluggish rivulets and grown with noxious weeds and clumps of coarse grass. Some distance away, a priest walked slowly, head bent, his double scalp lock flopping down over the radiant blue-green robe. Above him, apparently in communion with him, hung a golden globe.

Revel shifted his gun up and took aim at the orb. He must risk a shot, rather than a god's exposure of his whereabouts. The priest looked up, saw him, yipped in surprise, and the orb shot up ten feet just as Revel fired.

One bullet wasted. Jerran fired as the echoes of the Mink's shot racketed away, and the priest crumpled in on himself, a glittering sack of dead meat.

"You fool!" said Revel, with a brief, pithy anger. "The man I could have stabbed or broken in two. The sphere is beyond us now." It was slanting up an invisible incline, faster than he had ever seen one travel before. "Come on," he snarled. "We've got to travel!" He threw away the useless gun and ran for his life.

Behind him, to left and then to right, rose the calls. Hoofs thundered, dogs baying out afresh as they sighted their quarry, and the valley filled with sound and horses, dogs and men. Over and over the calls rang, and the air above the fugitives was filled with watching gods. Revel ran as he had never believed he could run, and the calls, the calls, the calls beat upon his eardrums...

CHAPTER TEN

The pretty daughter of the squire,
She gallops down the hill;
The blood of gentry pounds so fierce,
'Tis like to make her ill!

Thinks she, I've come to see his death,
The man who did me shame!
And then she spies him limping there,
All stripped and torn and lame...
    —Ruck's Ballad of the Mink

The squire was clad in a sky-blue velvet coat, long and loose with a row of big silver buttons down the front, a cabbage rose on each flared lapel, a thick fall of silver lace over an olive-green weskit, lime breeches in white calf boots. His blunderbuss was tilted carelessly up over one crooked elbow, for he trusted to the iron-shod hoofs of his hunting stallion to smash the rebel into the muck of the valley. He was a portly, floridly handsome man of some thirty summers, and he would not live to see the sun rise again.

Revel turned at bay. He was just under the overhang of a short cliff, on his right hand a swamp, on his left a pack of approaching hounds, and before him the squire on his upreared horse. He had just boosted Jerran up to the cliff's edge, and the little man was scrambling away, calling to him to follow; but there was no purchase for his fingers, and the thing was too high to jump, at least in the brief moment he had. So he was brought to bay.

The Mink drew his daggers, his fangs of Ewyo's more or less generous bestowal. The horse poised an instant before bringing its mallet-hoofs down on his head, and Revel leaped in and thrust—hands together, knuckles pressed tight, so that the blades drove deep into the flesh just below the rib cage of the stallion, their points not two inches apart. Revel jerked them apart and out, and the horse contorted and writhed together in a thrashing heap and came down, its blood hissing out from a foot-long gash. The squire, unable to realize what was happening, fell sideways on top of the Mink, who stabbed upward blindly as he rolled away from the dying horse. The squire took one dagger in the groin of his spotless lime breeches, the other just under a silver button above his heart. The world shut out for him in pain and terror and a loud, broken screech.

Revel fought out of the tangle of limbs and crumpled corpse, shot to his feet in time to meet the charge of a pair of slavering hounds. He knew he was done now, there was no more running for the Mink, and he cursed his fate even as he blessed whatever power had sent him so many gentry to be pulled down with him. The dogs leaped, one died in mid-air and the other carried him down once more, its lean teeth snapping off a patch of hide and muscle from his shoulder as its guts poured free of its body through a frantically-given wound. Revel was up again, shaking himself, grappling with a third hound whose knowledge of men made it wary of his blades. It hauled away as he slashed at it, lunged for his throat, caught an ear instead, and coughed out its life as it was flung over his shoulder in time for him to run the next dog through the skull as it sailed at him.

He was bleeding like a punctured sack of wine, though the wounds were far from mortal. One ear lobe was gone, his left shoulder felt as though it had been scalded by boiling pitch, and his whole frame was stiffening somewhat from the myriad tiny cuts it had received. Revel was in his glory, although he counted his life in seconds now. The whole pack was not in the valley, these four dogs had not run with it, and only men remained. Yet above were the orbs, to take a hand if he should prove too mighty for the gentry's handling.

A squire galloped up, jumped from his saddle and came at the Mink. Revel blinked blood from his eyes.

"Rosk!" he said, grinning. Now the gods were kind!

The lean-jawed squire halted twenty feet away, presenting his gun to the Mink's breast. "A fine fox," he said admiringly, "a damned fine fox, but too vicious for the hounds. Die, Mink!"

"Damned if I will," said Revel, flinging himself forward and down. The gun roared harmlessly as Rosk, startled, tugged on the trigger. Revel went up to stab for the man's belly, but a warning tremor of the ground gave him pause; a stallion was thundering down on him from the left. He flicked a glance at it. A great roan, with the Lady Nirea up, and coming straight for him.

She would run him down? He bared angry teeth—but she was going to miss him! She was galloping between him and Rosk! She was...

She was stretching down a hand to him, her face twisted with hope and fear and—friendship!

Instinctively he slapped her wrist with his palm as she hurtled past, jerked his legs up and was carried off by the rocketing roan. As he writhed into the saddle behind her, she screamed.

"Help, oh help! He has attacked me!"

The clever girl, by Orbs! Helping him, she was yet saving her own reputation and life, making it seem that he had leaped astride her mount as she was carried by him. No squire could have seen that helping hand, for they were all on the opposite side of her. A vast hullabaloo went up from their ranks.

"Throw me off, you fool," she hissed at him, twisting round and pretending to strike him. "Throw me off!"

He reached past her, hauled on the reins, brought the animal back on its heels, pitched her off unceremoniously, winked broadly at her and found time for a leer as her riding skirt hoisted unladylike as she sat up; then he rammed heels to the brute and was off on a run for his life. Guns banged behind him, slugs tore the air inches from his bowed back. Let 'em shoot, curse them, he had a chance now!

The cliff of reed-laced muck dwindled, and he turned the roan and leaped him up to the higher level of ground. Then he turned and went charging back the way he had come, quick eyes searching for his comrade.

"Jerran! Jerran, you scuttling mouse, where are you?"

Bang went a musket.

"Here, Revel!" The little straw-colored man popped out of a bush in his path. He bent as Nirea had, gave the rebel a hand up behind him. Then he swerved the horse and went off through the oaks, while the gentry cursed and raved and came after as best they could.

"Discomfortable riding, this, without pants. Ouch! Where shall we head, ancient one?" Revel asked grimly.

"The way we're going. There, see that hill? Up and over that, and we're on a straight path for the forests of Kamden."

Revel was jolted nearly out of his battered hide by the unfamiliar jounce and rock of the steed; but he knew he could stick on it till night if he had to. The only enemies that fretted him now were the golden spheres. You could not distance a god simply by mounting a horse.

"Look up," he said, watching the path. "Are there gods?"

"Yes, but high, following us. They mark our way."

"Let them! Jerran, at nightfall we head for the mine. Our mine, and our cavern."

"You can't go there, you drooling baby, you'd find an army of globes, priests, gentry, and zanphs. They'll be crawling all over the things in that cave, especially after you took guns from it! What is it that draws you there?"

"A metal chest—ouch—I've been thinking of for a long time. Jerran, what's 'suspended animation'?"

"Why?"

"Nirea kept muttering it to herself in the cave. I think she read it on the chest."

"Suspended," mused Jerran. "Temporarily halted. Animation, life. Life held in check? Movement stopped for a time?"

"That's it."

"Love of freedom, lad, what's it?"

Revel, glancing up at the soaring spheres, said half to himself, "Man of the 21st century. A century is a hundred years…a hundred years. Twenty-first? John R. Klapham, atomic something…suspended animation. John sounds like a name. Rest of it, enigmas, but…"

"Watch out!" yelled Jerran, turning against his back. "A god comes at us."

"How good are you at throwing knives?"

"As good as the next rebel. Damned good."

"Take one from my belt, and see if you can spit it in the air. If it touches you, you'll be a frizzled-up cinder in a wink."

He felt the knife leave his holster, there was a pause, then Jerran said under her breath, "Blast this horse— ugh—got it!"

They were almost at the crest of the hill now. None of the ruck watched the chase from here, for it was far from Ewyo's house and none had expected Revel and Company to come so far. There were guards, though: three squires sitting their quiet horses on the brow of the hills, a hundred yards apart. They watched the roan with its double burden beat up toward them, then blinked and peered as they saw that the foremost rider was naked.

"Va-yoo," said one uncertainly, then, realization hitting him, "va-yoo hallo! Here he comes!"

He came, and the squires bunched to meet him; he aimed his horse's head for their center, they split off wildly at the last instant, and he was through them before they could draw guns from the saddle boots. A crack behind him was the first one speaking tardily, and the roan leaped forward, touched into fury by the slug's creasing its withers. Jerran said calmly, "I'm hit in the leg. Let me see. A flesh wound, no matter. Ride, lad!"

"The globes are our only worries now," said Revel exultantly.

"And they're some worries, for they descend even now at us."

He looked up, and saw that it was true. A multitude of the radiant gods were dropping from their buttons, and the forest of Kamden with its sprawling borders and its secret, protective darknesses lay half a mile before the Mink.

Almost he would rather have died by a squire's bullet than a pseudo-god's fierce energy blast. He recalled the feelers that had touched his face yesterday, the searing heat of the aura that before that had crisped off the hair above his ear. It was a filthy way to die.

The roan, strongest of all the gentry's horses, was easily distancing them all. But it could not distance a down-slanting globe.

Revel the Mink committed his soul to whatever might receive it, and dug in his heels for a last desperate gallop.

CHAPTER ELEVEN

The ruckers all have heard the call
The Mink has sounded clear;
They come from near, they come from far,
To fight the squire and sphere.

He arms them all with stolen guns,
With horses, pikes, and fire;
He sends them all abroad to hunt
The savage-stallioned squire!
        —Ruck's Ballad of the Mink

As night fell, Lady Nirea left her father's house by the servants' door. She was dressed in the miner's clothes she had worn the previous day, and carried a gigantic portmanteau, so heavy she could scarcely lift it.

In the bag were her favorite gowns, numbering sixteen; two coats she especially loved; some bracelets set with diamonds—the rarest gem of any, for though they were mined extensively throughout the country, the globes took all but a very few for their own mysterious purposes—and an antique golden chain she'd inherited from her grandmother; some personal effects, paint for her lips and such frivolities; a trumpet-mouthed gun with the stock unmounted, together with as much ammunition as she could find; and lastly, four books from her father's secret chamber.

These last were all in the curious run-together printing, three of them labelled "Ledger and Record Book" and the fourth with "God-Feeding" on its cover. The fourth was far older than the others, indeed, the oldest book Nirea had ever seen.

Ewyo lay drunk in a deep chair in his library; he would sleep now till nearly the middle of the night, when he'd wake up and howl for another bottle. Jann she had not seen for hours. The servants, being ruckers, did not count. Her escape from the mansion was going to be simple.

In the stables, Lady Nirea ordered her second best horse, another roan stallion, saddled and laden with the portmanteau on a special rack attached to the rear of the cantle. The usual trappings, the fancy reins and broidered saddlecloths, she had the stableman leave off; she didn't want to call attention to the fact that she was Ewyo's daughter.

When the roan was ready, she mounted, and turning to the stableman, a young rucker with shifty eyes and a shy, retiring chin, she asked steadily, "Are you a rebel?"

"Me? No, Lady! Do I look crazy?"

"You look sneaky, but smart enough." She leaned over the saddlebow toward him. "Tell me the truth. Don't be afraid, you fool. I am the Lady of the Mink." It was a title she uttered proudly now. Nirea of Dolfya had been forced to think this day, and it had changed her greatly.

The stableman backed off a little, his pasty face writhing with tics. "My Orb, Lady, I don't know what you're thinking of! You, Ewyo's girl, calling yourself such a name—"

Her roan was trained to the work she now put him to; a number of times she'd used him for it in the streets of Dolfya, just for sport, out of boredom. Now she pricked his ribs with the point of her sharp-toed shoes, just behind the foreleg joints, and said, "At 'em, boy!" The tall beast reared up and danced forward, hoofs thrashing the air. The stableman shrieked, took a step back, and threw up his arms as one iron-shod hoof smashed into his face. Then the roan was doing a kind of quick little hop on his body, and red blood ran out over the packed-earth floor.

"If you were a rebel, you were too craven about it to be much good to your people," Nirea said, looking at the body. "If you weren't, then your mouth is shut concerning me." She wheeled the roan and trotted out of the stable.

By the gate in the wall a tall figure waited, white in the early moon's light.

"Jann!" said Nirea, with surprise and fear. Her older sister had always bullied her; Nirea was unable to wholly conquer the dread of this amber-eyed, sharp-eared woman. Jann stood with one hand on the gate, her high breasts and lean aristocrat's profile outlined against the dark black-green of the woods behind her. Now she turned her head to look up at Nirea.

"What in the seven hells are you doing in that rucker's outfit? Where are you going?"

"None of your business. Get out of my way."

Jann stepped forward and grasped the bridle at the roan's mouth. "Get down here, you young whelp. I'm going to beat you—and then hand you over to Ewyo to see what's to be done with you."

Nirea never knew, though afterwards she thought of it often, whether she touched her horse's ribs deliberately or by accident. All she knew was that suddenly he had thrown his forequarters up into the air, that Jann was screaming, twisting aside, that the roan was smashing down...

Jann lay on the grass, and her profile was no longer aristocratic; nor were her breasts smooth and sleek and inviolate.

Nirea sobbed, dry-eyed, turned the roan away, leaned over to push open the gate, and cantered off down the silent road, numb with horror, yet conscious of a small thrill of gratification, somewhere deep in her feral gentrywoman's soul. Nineteen years of knuckling under to Jann, of taking insults and cuffs and belittling, were wiped out under the flashing hoofs of her roan stallion.

Now where should she ride? She was a rebel herself, molded into one by her father's actions and her memories of the Mink. If he were dead, that great chocolate-haired brute, then she would simply ride straight away from Dolfya until she found a place to live, and there plan at leisure. But if he were alive, then she would be his woman.

She touched the horse to a gallop, and sped toward the only place she could think of where she might get news of him: the mines.

Someone scuttled off the road before her; she reined in, peered unsuccessfully into the darkness, and called softly, insistently, "If you're a rucker, please come out!   Please come here!"

A rustle in dry brush was her answer. She tried a bolder tack. "It's the Lady of the Mink who commands it!"

After a moment a man stepped onto the road from a clump of bracken.   Red were his hair and beard in the moon, and the white walleye stared blindly. Fate, chance, the gods—no, not the false, horrible globes, but whatever gods there might be elsewhere—had crossed her path with Rack, the giant whom she trusted more than any other rucker.

"Rack!" she called quietly. "Come here, man."

He was at her stirrup. "What are you doing, Lady?" His voice was anxious:

"I'm joining the rebels, big man. Where can I find the Mink?"

"I don't know. Lady, are you mad? The rebels are saying that the gods are overthrown and there will be gentry blood running all over Dolfya by noon tomorrow. They're out of their heads."

"No, Rack, they're honest men fighting a hideous corruption." She told him rapidly what she'd seen in her father's room. "I don't know exactly what it means, 'but it's bad—degrading, horrible!   I don't want to be a gentrywoman any longer. I—I'm the Mink's girl. Listen," she said, leaning over to him, "he took me two days ago, and Revel is my man, hell or orbs notwithstanding. Now where is he?"

"I've heard he's alive," said Rack slowly. "I thought he would be; he's too tough to kill. Where he is, no one knows."

"Do the rebels trust you?"

"No." His face turned up to hers, honest and bewildered. "I'm of two minds... I serve the gods, as any sane man must, but I have seen things..."

"So have I. Rack, come with me. We must find the Mink."

He bit his lip. Then he took hold of her stirrup. She thought he was going to pull her off, and edged her toes forward toward the signal points of her roan; but he merely said, "I'll hang on to this and run. Go ahead, Lady."

She tapped the horse to a canter, feeling better than she had in hours. Rack was a servant (say rather an ally) worth four other men.

"Head for the mines," grunted Rack. Her own idea. Surely it must be worth something. Soon they were coming into the coal valley. God-guards shone with an eerie and now-abominable golden light at the various entrances. "Which is Revel's?" she asked.

"Up there. He wouldn't be there, but if I can get past the guard, and there's no reason I should be stopped, there are men on our level, the fourth down, who might know about him. There's no other place to check. I don't know the meeting places. I have never been a rebel." He seemed to brood darkly for a minute, then added, "Before!"

They hobbled the horse in a nook of upended rocks, and she hid the portmanteau under some brush. They walked to the mine, she now remembering the location by certain landmarks, and Rack said, "There's no god showing. That's strange."

"I'll go with you as far as I can. If we do meet a god, I can explain myself mentally; after all, I'm of the gentry. I'm not in danger."

"I hope not." He helped her up the shelf, and they walked furtively into the tunnel. No sign of anything—till Rack stumbled over the corpse of a zanph. Bending, Nirea saw beyond it the sack and draining ichor of a globe.

"The rebels have been here!"

"Aye." He straightened, his white eye shining in the light of a distant lantern. "How can a god die?" he asked, in a child's puzzled tone. "Lady, no god ever died before. They don't die—'tis in the Credo. How can these rebels slay them?"

"Maybe no one ever tried before. Come on." She hurried to the ladders. Blue-tinged, mouth agape and eyes upturned without sight, there lay a priest, half over the lip of the shaft. He had been de-throated by a pickax.

"This looks like Revel's ferocious work," said Rack. "I hope he's alive. Yes, I do hope so."

"When I last saw him, riding off hell-for-leather on my nag, he was extremely alive, mother-naked and covered with blood but as alive as I am this instant." She went down the ladder hand under hand past three levels, swung off at the fourth. Another dead man lay at her feet; this was a squire, a youngish man in plum and scarlet, very brutally slain by a pick-slash in the brain. It was a man she knew, and momentarily she felt herself a traitor to her kind; then she thought of Ewyo's vices, corruptions, and she snorted defiantly. His gun, its stock remounted and a shell rammed home, was in her hand. She went forward, striding like a man...and a man who knew what he meant to do.

The end of the tunnel was illuminated vividly by many blue lanterns, and presented to their startled eyes an horrific scene of carnage. The dead lay in piles, in one and twos and fours, their brains splashed on the walls, their guts smeared across the floor, their skulls cloven and their bodies rent. Ruckers lay here, miners and gentry-servants. Squires wallowed lifeless in pools of their highborn blood. Snake-headed zanphs clawed in their rigor at the dead flesh of priests, of rebels, of squires. Here and there lay the vacant sacks that had been gods. At Nirea's feet stretched a man built like Revel, who might *be* Revel, for his face was gone, burnt away by the touch of the terrible orb-aura at full strength. No, she realized even as she swayed back, it was not he, for this man's body was unscarred, and Revel must be looking like a skinned hare if he yet lived.

What a brawl this must have been! She was about to speak to Rack when she heard a familiar voice, booming brazenly out in the silence of the mine. It came from the black hole at the end of the tunnel.

"Then a whole line of them came down at us, faster than a squire can put a horse over a hurdle, and the forest yet a good half mile away! I had one dagger left, and my trusty small Jerran up behind me. The squires were ashooting, but ineffectively, and the roan was carrying us well and truly; but here came the gods, may they boil in my mother's cook-pot in Hell!

"I looked wildly for something to beat 'em off with, for as you've seen, a touch of their radiance burns your flesh from your bones if they wish it so. Well! The only thing on the whole cursed nag is the scabbard in which a squire keeps his long gun. It's a thing some three feet long or over, of light metal, covered with satin and velvet and silk. I tore it from its moorings, and as the globes came at me, I stood up in the stirrups, naked as your hand, and started to swat 'em. Jerran leaning forward past me, guiding the stallion, for his reach is not half mine."

"Brag and bounce!" said a voice that was surely Jerran's. Lady Nirea grinned and walked toward the cavern.

"So I swatted, I beat at them, I swiped and almost fell, I did the work of twenty men—don't shake your head, Jerran, you know 'tis not brag!—for half a mile, and not one globe touched a hair of our heads! They came at the last from all sides, like a swarm of angered bees, and one burnt the horse so that he streaked even faster; which saved our necks, for my arm was nearly dead by then.

"I tell you, there is one protection only against these things, and that is quickness: for let one come within a few inches of you, and you are a dead man."

Nirea stepped into the cave.

"I thought you were a dead man, Revel the Mink," she said quietly, still with the ghost of her grin.

He stared at her, while the men in the place turned and sprang up and stood uncertainly, looking from her to their leader. He was dressed in miner's clothing again, and his skin was a perfect fright of scars and scabs and half-closed wounds. But he was whole, barring part of an ear, and he was smiling as only he could smile. "Here, men of the ruck, is the woman you owe my life to. Here is—" he cocked an eyebrow quizzically— "here is, I think I can say, the Lady of the Mink."

"Here she is," said Nirea, and was stifled and crushed in a great bear-hug. "And here's Rack, your brother, who I think may be rebel material."

"I think so," said Rack heavily, staring at Revel with his good eye. "If you want me, brother."

"Gods, yes! We need every man we can get this night. Did you note the slaughter beyond?"

"We did see a corpse or two."

"I think we kept that secret, for two of my fellows stood on the ladders and slew the gods who tried to pass. But it will soon be discovered, and the gods will do to this place what they did to eastern Dolfya, unless we can fight them some way. I think I have a clue to help us. What that is I'll show you now."

"Revel, dearest," she said, "are you all right?"

"Of course, thanks to you. Now to business."

"Rack must go to my horse above for things I brought."

"Go then, Rack. Wait—first give me that pick you've got there. I think it's mine." Rack handed it over, a little shamefacedly, and Revel gave him the one tucked in his own belt. "I've missed this girl... The chest I want to search is still here, though the gentry have carried off a great deal from the cavern."

"Wait a minute," said Nirea fiercely. "You'd better do a few things before you start experimenting and searching. You'd better have a plan, and send men out to spread word of it among your people! There are thousands of them out there, ready to pounce at your word, to rise against the squires and priests, and take their chances of gods' vengeance. You'd better send out the word that the Mink is leading them to war. Otherwise, you'll have an army that's ineffectual and headless, that can be cut to pieces in twenty-four hours. For most of them think you're dead— the gentry spread the word."

Jerran said, quietly so that only the girl and Revel heard him, "I think I named the wrong person. I think Lady Nirea is the Mink!"

Revel laughed grimly, "Haven't I been busy? Haven't I sent a troop for Dawvys in his hole in the coppice, and another to say in the lanes and shebeens that I'm alive? Here, Vorl, Sesker, and you three, get out! Steal horses from the mansions' stables, and spread the news. We rise tonight! Whether or not I find what I seek, we rise! If we all perish in a god-blast, still we rise! When you've enough men, attack the gentry's homes, beginning at Dolfya's center and spreading out. Put every horse available on the road to Korla and Hakes Town and every village within knowledge. If they look scared, show 'em a dead god! Take those out there—stick 'em on the ends of pikes, carry 'em through the streets with torches to show 'em off! Kill every globe you can reach, send the corpses out for the ruck to see! There's our banner, our fiery cross—a dead god on a pike!"

CHAPTER TWELVE

The gods have looked upon the Mink,
And felt his mighty hand;
They've sought him through the mines and towns,
And in the forest land.

All-wise, all-powerful though they be,
The Mink they cannot find;
Afar he's wandering o'er the earth,
At war for all mankind.
    —Ruck's Ballad of the Mink

"Read it again," said Revel, bending his scarred face beside the girl's sleek one, staring hard at the printing as if by concentration on it he could learn to read right there, and drag the hidden meaning from the words. "Read slowly. Rack, you're no slouch at thought, even though you have been in the toils of the false gods. Give this your best brainwork. Jerran, concentrate! You three men, try to cull the sense from these words. Begin!"

In the light of half a dozen lanterns she began to read. The Mink strained all his brains.

"*Man of the 21st century: John R. Klapham, atomic physicist and leader of the Ninth Expedition against the Tartarian Forces in the year 2054. Held in suspended animation.*"

"Ha! I thought that's where you got the phrase," said Revel. "I believe it means that in this chest, and thank Orbs it was too heavy for the gentry to move today, in this very chest lies a man of the Ancient Kingdom, who still lives, though he sleeps!"

The woman looked up excitedly, then began to read again. Most of the words were strange. "Placed here 10-5-2084, aged 64 years; this done voluntarily and as a public service to the men of the future, as part of the program of living interments inaugurated in 2067."

"Living interments," repeated Rack heavily. "Buried alive. But you think he still lives?"

"I think so. Don't ask me why I simply do. The words burn my brain."

"What are the numbers?" asked a miner. "2067, the year 2054—what are they?"

"I don't know. Go on, Nirea."

"Instructions for opening the casket: spring back the locks along each bottom edge." She felt the chest where it rested on six legs on the floor. "Here are odd-shaped things—ooh!" She jerked her hand away. "They leap at me!"

Revel felt impatiently, said, "Those are the locks." He unsnapped fourteen altogether. "What next?"

"Run a knife along the seal two inches below the top."

"Here's the seal," said Rack. He took his pick, and thrusting the point of it into a soft metal strip that ran around the chest, tore it away with one long hard tug. The Mink finished the job on sides and back; "Read!" he said.

"Lift off the top." She glanced at Revel. "This is almost exactly like Orbish," she said. "Only those queer words—"

"Philosophize in the corner," he said, pushing her aside. "Rack, lend me your brawn." Together they lifted the top, which was about the weight of a woods lion, and with much groaning and puffing, hurled it clear.

Below them, within the chest and under a sheet of the transparent stuff they had seen in other parts of the cave, lay a man. He was young-looking, though if Revel understood the words on the chest, he had been sixty-four when he was hidden away here. His skin was brown, smooth, and his closed eyes were unwrinkled. A short oddly-cut beard of brindled gray and black fringed his chin. His hands, folded on the chest, were big and sinewy, fighter's hands.

"What now?" panted Revel.

"Provided that the atmosphere is still a mixture of 21 parts oxygen to 78 parts nitrogen, with 1% made of small amounts of the gases neon, helium, krypton—none of these words make sense."

"Skip them, then. Find something that does."

"Let's see…swing the front of the casket up, and unhinge it so that it comes off." They figured out what was meant, and did it. The front of the metal case, very light compared with the top, fell with a clang. "Insert a crowbar under the glass that covers the man and lift it carefully away."

"Crowbar? Glass?"

"This almost invisible stuff covers him, it must be the 'glass'," said Jerran. "Let's try to lift it off."

It took Revel and Rack and two miners, but in a matter of five minutes, they had removed the plate of glass, the thin curved sheet that had protected this man of the Ancient Kingdom. "Next?"

"Provided that it is no later than the year 3284, Doctor Klapham should revive within an hour. If not, take the hypodermic from the white case below him and inject 2cc... Do you understand this at all?" she asked.

"Only that the man, whose name is evidently Doctor Klapham, ought to wake up shortly." The Mink shook his great brown head. "If only we'd found this cave in a quiet time! If only the gods and the gentry weren't to be dealt with! Have we the time?"

"Your work is going on above-ground," said Jerran, rubbing his chin. "We can't be of more use anywhere else, it seems to me, than we may be right here."

They sat and watched the inert form of Doctor Klapham, while two of their rebels went out into the mine to round up anyone who would join them. In something over half an hour they were back. "The mine's been cleared; nothing anywhere except this man, who was on the lowest level and hasn't heard a thing."

"They missed me, I guess," said the newcomer. "I was off in an abandoned tunnel sleeping."

"We're eight, then." The Mink scratched his head reflectively. "Not a bad fighting force. Provided they don't smear this whole valley, I think we can win clear—after we see what this fellow is going to do."

"I think I see him breathing," said the girl breathlessly. She was sitting with a book on her lap, trying to decipher the meaning of its words. "Look at his throat."

Doctor Klapham made a strange sound in his chest, a clicking, quite audible noise, and unfolding his strong hands, sat up.

"Well," he said clearly, "didn't it work?" Then he took a closer look at the eight people standing beside him. "Oh, my Lord," he said, "it *did* work!"

"He speaks Orbish," said Rack, "but with a different accent. Could he be from the far towns?"

"No, you idiot, from the Ancient Kingdom," said Revel. "Your name is Doctor Klapham, isn't it?"

"Roughly, yes." The sleeper worked his jaws and massaged his hands. "Wonderful stuff, that preservative…what year is this, my friend?"

"I don't know what you mean."

"What's the date?"

"Date?"

"God, this I wasn't prepared for." He hoisted himself over and jumped down with boyish energy. "Tell me about the world," he said. "I guess I've been asleep a long time."

"Yes, if you were put here in the time of the Ancient Kingdom." Revel was trembling with excitement. "Why are you still alive?"

"Friend, judging from your clothes and those picks, and the primitive look of those lanterns, which must date from about 2015, I'd say it'd be pretty useless to tell you how come I'm alive. Just call it science."

"What's that?"

"Science? Electronics, atomic research, mechanics, what have you—mean anything?"

"I'm sorry," said the Mink, "no."

"You speak quite decent English, you know. It's funny it hasn't changed much, unless I've been asleep a lot shorter a period than I figure."

"My language is Orbish."

"It's English to me. What's the name of your country, son?"

"It has no name. Towns are named, not countries."

"Who are you, then?"

"I am Revel, the Mink," he said proudly. "I am the leader of the rebels, who are even now spreading through the land sending the word that the gods can die, and that the gentry's day is done. I am the Mink."

He half-expected the man to know the old ballads, but Doctor Klapham said, "Mink? That was an animal when I was around last... Call me John."

"John. That sounds like a name." Rack nodded. "Yes, this is better than Doctor Klapham."

"Anybody have a cigarette?" asked John.

"What's that?"

"A fag, boy—tobacco, something to smoke. You drag it in and puff it out."

"Your words make no sense," said Revel. "Drag in smoke?"

"This is going to be worse than I anticipated," said John. "Look, can't we go somewhere and get comfortable? I have a lot to find out before I can start getting across to you what I was sent into the future for."

"We are besieged by the gods. We dare not leave this place."

"By the gods. Hmm. Let's sit down, boy. I want to know all about things here. Miss, after you." He waited till Nirea had squatted on the floor, then folded himself down.

"Okay," he said, whatever that meant. "Shoot. Begin. What are the gods, first?"

Lady Nirea listened with half an ear to Revel's speeches, but with all her intellect she tried to follow John's remarks. They were sometimes fragmentary, sometimes short explanations of things that puzzled Revel, and sometimes merely grunts and slappings of his thighs. Many words she did not know...

My God, that sounds like extraterrestrial beings...globes, golden aura of energy or force, sure, that's possible; and tentacles...zanphs? describe 'em...they aren't from Earth either; I'll bet you these god-globes of yours, which must be Martian or Venusian or Lord-knows-what, brought along those pretty pets when they hit for Earth...

Listen, Mink, those are not gods! They're things from the stars, from out there beyond the world! You understand that? They came here in those "buttons" of yours—what we used to call flying saucers—and took over after...after whatever happened. Your civilization must have been in a hell of a decline to accept 'em as gods, because in my day...oh, well, go ahead.

Priests, sure, there'd be a class of sycophants, bastards who'd sell out to the extraterrestrials for glory and profit...yeah, your gentry sound like another type of sell-out, traitors to their race and their world...describe those squires' costumes again, will you? Holy cats, eighteenth century to a T! Not a thread changed, from the sound of it! And a lower class, you call it the ruck, which is downtrodden and lives in what might as well be hell...

Yep, it sure sounds like hell and ashes. The globes; then, as is natural to a conquered country, the top dogs, priests in your case, who run things but are run by the globes; then the privileged gentry—I'll have a look at those books of yours in a minute, honey—who pay some kind of tax, in money or sweat or produce or something, for being what they are; then the ruck (I know the word, son, you've just enlarged its meaning) who have been serfs and peasants and vassals and thralls and churls and hoi polloi and slaves since the Egyptians crawled out of the Nile. The great unwashed, the people. Let 'em eat cake. I'm sorry, Mink, go on.

Your gentry sound about as lousy a pack of hellions as the eighteenth century squires! Too bad you don't know about tobacco, they could carry snuffboxes and really act the part...

My God! Even the fox hunts—with people hunted. Anyone but miners? Open days, eh? Ho-oly...

Glad to know you, Rack. Don't know as I'd care to have you on the other side, you look like Goliath. So you just saw the light when the gods started to die? You are lucky you saw it, big man; brother against brother is the nastiest form of war, especially if mankind's fighting an alien power...

Your rebels sound familiar, Mink. They had 'em about like you in Ireland, a hundred or so years ago—I mean before I went bye-bye... Always romantic, unbelievable, unfindable, foxes with fangs...

I wonder what your globes wanted? Power, sure, if they're that humanoid in concept, but it must have been more. Maybe their own planet blew up. Maybe they ran out of something. Tell me, do you have to give them anything? Any metal, say?

Diamonds? Are those small hard chunks of—yes, I guess diamond still means what it did. By gravy, I'll bet I know! They were just starting to discover the terrific potential of energy of the diamond when I went to sleep in 2084. I wonder how long ago that was? Anyway, I'll wager these globes of yours run their damned saucers—buttons—on diamond energy. Maybe their planet ran out of diamonds. By god! what a yarn!

You'll have your hands full, but maybe I can help. There's a way to bring those saucers down out of the sky in a hurry... They won't give up easily. They obviously have atomic bombs, and the lush intoxication of power won't be a cinch to give up, not for anything that sounds as egotistic as the globes...

Dolfya? We called it Philadelphia. Kamden, Camden, yeah... Woods lions, wow! They must be mutants from zoo or circus lions that escaped during the atom wars; or maybe someone brought 'em to the U.S. The Tartarians had tame lions, I remember.

Six or eight brains? Well, Mink, I wouldn't argue, but I think you are confusing certain functions of one brain with—oh, do go on!

Let me see that gun. My Lord, what a concoction! Blunderbuss muzzle, shells, yet no breech-loading; ramrods to shove in shells! My sainted aunt! A fantastic combination...

He eats dandelions, parsley, grass, eh...chlorophyll, obviously. And the globe rests on his chest and puts tentacles into his mouth and nostrils. It's feeding, sure; look at the title of this book you've got here. This is a bastard English but close enough. Certainly your father wrote it, Miss. Some of your gentry must have preserved the art as a secret.

Look here: I'll make it as plain as I can. The globes are from another world. They came here for diamonds to run their buttons with. Got that?

Now here's what I deduce from the little I've read here. Talk about Pepy's Diary! Hadn't anything on this chronicle. Your father and the other gentry have to feed the globes periodically. Evidently they draw nourishment out of the human bodies—all that chlorophyll makes me think it's a definitely physical nourishment, rather than a psychic one. That's what your people pay for being privileged powers in the land. They stand the disgrace and the pain, if there is any, the draining of their energies, in return for plain old magnetic power.

So that's the source of life, strength, what-have-you, of the aliens! They must have gotten pretty frantic out in the space wastes, looking for a planet that could afford them a life form that was tap-able.

Evidently it has to be voluntary, from these books. I guess the ancestors of the ruck had their crack at the honor and declined, thus dooming themselves and their offspring to servitude; while those that assented became the gentry. What a—Judas Priest! What a sordid state of affairs for poor old Earth!

Let me have that line from the Globate Credo again: They came from the sky before our grandfathers were born, to a world torn by war; they settled our differences and raised us from the slime—*there's a bitter laugh, gentlemen*—giving us freedom. All we have we owe to the globes. *There's the whole tale in a nutshell. God!*

Orbish language, Orbuary, Orbsday—nice job they did of infiltrating. I wonder what books they left you. I'd like a look at your father's library. Alice in Wonderland, I suppose, or Black Beauty, or something equally advanced.

Now listen, lads, and you, Lady Nirea. I came from a world that may have had its rugged spots, but it was heaven and Utopia compared with this one. You disinterred me at the damndest most vital moment of your history, and probably of Earth's as well—we've had conquerors aplenty, but always of this world, not from out of it. It seems to me that if your rebellion fails, you're due for worse treatment than ever. You've got to win, and win fast. Any entity that has atomic weapons is going to be no easy mark, and the gentry have guns. How about you people? Ten? Ten guns altogether? Oohh…

See here. That big machine over there is a—well, that's hopeless. I'll try to break this down in one-syllable words. Orbish words, I hope.

That big thing sends up rays like beams of sunlight but of different intensity, color, wave length, et cetera—it sends up beams that counteract, I mean work against, destroy, other beams. Now the buttons are held up there by forces in diamonds, taken out by these globes of yours and used to hold up their homes, ships, saucers, buttons. The beams from that big thing will destroy the diamond beams and make the buttons fall.

There's just one thing. We have to get the machine, the thing, out of this cave and onto the surface of the earth. You catch my meaning? It has to have sky above it before it can work against the button-beams. Yes, much like your globes' telepathy (what a word to survive, when "glass" and "electricity" didn't) and hypnosis fails when rock gets in the way.

Can you get it to the surface? Talk it over, Mink. It can give you plenty of help...if you can get it up there. I'll just sit here, if it's okay with you, and let my imagination boggle at what you've told me.

I have the most confounded urgent feeling that this is a visit I'm making in a time machine, and that tomorrow I'll go back to good old 2084. Johnnie, Johnnie, wake up! You're here!

God!

CHAPTER THIRTEEN

The Mink he takes his pick and gun,
He ranges through the towns;
His force is miners, trappers, thieves—
And a girl in gentry-gown.

The rebels ride on stolen nags,
They travel on shanks' mare;
The gore's awash, the heads they roll,
All in the torches' glare.
      —Ruck's Ballad of the Mink

Revel the Mink and his eight troops crouched in the dark entrance of the mine. The night was black, clouds had obscured the moon, and only the occasional pinpoints of globes drifting between the buttons above them broke the gloom.

"What are they doing?" hissed Nirea. "Why haven't we been attacked long since?"

"The globes move in a mysterious way their wonders to perform," muttered John Klapham. "I'll wager there's something like that in the Globate Credo."

"Almost those words." Revel glanced at him respectfully. This man of the Ancient Kingdom had great mental powers.

"Sure. Every time somebody has the upper hand over somebody else, there's got to be an aura of mystery; and any half-brained action is put down to 'mysterious ways'." He spat. "They're so damn confused, son, that they're probably holding forty conferences up there, because they don't dare wipe out this valley—coal keeps the gentry warm and happy for 'em—and they want to inspect the cave down below. So they're tryin' to think of the best way to squelch you without losing too many priests and zanphs and gentry."

"True, they mustn't lose too many servants, or their prestige is hurt," said Lady Nirea. Now that she'd found her Revel, she had discarded the rucker's clothing and was dressed in a thigh-hugging sapphire gown. Even in the dark she was beautiful, he thought.

The Mink stood. Up and down the valley glowed the lights of god-guards at the mines, double and treble now, since with the Mink loose not even a god was safe alone. Plenty of zanphs there too, he thought. Yet he had a few gentryman's guns, and his old pick slung at his back. Zanphs, gods, gentry, priests? Let them beware!

His thinking was done; he would retire his brains—despite the clever John, Revel knew he had more than one brain—and let his brawn take over. Only the brawn of the Mink could win through the next hours. Half-consciously he tensed his whole frame, curled his fingers and toes, thrust out his great chest. The skin on all parts of his body creaked, split back from the worse wounds, achily stretched; blood sprang from shoulder and from other hurt places. Yet he was not only whole, but full of eager vitality. The small pains of his hide were only incentives to act violently and forget them. He relaxed and turned to his friends.

"You two, find the nags of the gentry we slew. I hear stamping nearby. Nirea, go to your own beast and wait for me. You two, with Rack, Jerran, John and me, we'll search the mines for men. We need plenty of them—it's miners' guts and muscles it'll take to move that beam-throwing thing from the cavern. Let's begin."

He drew the Lady Nirea up to him, slapped her face lightly, kissed her open mouth. "Quick, wench, hop when I speak!" A touch of starshine glistened on his grin-bared teeth. Then he turned and leaped off the rock shelf.

The nearest mine was guarded by three gods, nervously jiggling up and down in grotesque little air-dances; below them sat half a dozen hideous-headed zanphs. Revel crawled up toward the entrance. At the first touch of an alien mind on his own, he shot forward, pick flailing. Two gods he caught with one stroke, the third began to rise and his backswing took it on the underside and tore a gash as if the pick had struck a rubber bag: yellow gore dropped in a flood. He had no time to wonder if the third globe had telepathed a distress signal, for the zanphs were on him.

Their snake-like heads were fitted with only two teeth in each jaw, yet those were four inches long and thick as a man's thumb at the base, tapering to needle points. One zanph, propelled by all the vigor of its six legs, rose like a rocketing pheasant and clamped its jaws across his left arm.

It overshot, and two teeth missed; but the others dug down into the flesh and grated on the ulna bone.

He gave it a jab of the handle of his pickax between its cold pupilless eyes, and it swung limp, losing consciousness but anchored to his arm by the frightful teeth. He cracked the neck of another zanph with his foot, spitted a third, and then Rack and Jerran were slaying the others. John appeared and lifted the first one's body so that Revel could disengage the teeth from his bloody arm.

"What a beastie," marveled the Ancient Kingdom man. "How I'd love to dissect one!" Revel, puzzling over the word "dissect," went into the mine.

"Jerran, come along. You others remain, and keep off any intruders."

There were but three levels in this mine, and he covered them rapidly, Jerran at his heels. He slew seven more spheres, with four zanphs. His blood was up and his tongue lolled with excitement.

To his banner, which was a dead god on Jerran's pick, there came forty-three miners. Four others declined, and were allowed to stay at their posts, true to their false gods and the service of the gentry.

Coming out of this mine, he led a small army, and felt like a conquering general already. In two hours he had invaded every shaft in the valley, and six hundred men less a score or so were at his back.

"How's this for a start?" he asked Nirea, meeting her walking her roan on the grass. She glanced at the mass of men, all those in the van carrying dead globes. "Not bad...but have you seen the sky, Mink?"

He looked upward. From horizon to horizon the sky was ablaze with circles of light, red and green and violet, pure terrible white and flickering yellow. *The buttons*, murmured his men behind him. *The buttons are awake!*

"You couldn't expect to do it in secret, Revel," said John. The old man was as spry and eager as a boy, thought the Mink. "Now let's not waste time. I'm banking that the invaders, I mean the globes, won't blast this valley except as a last resort; if they read my mind, or if their science has gone far enough for 'em to recognize an anti-force-screen thrower when they see one, then we're practically atom soup now."

Revel, having understood at least one portion of the speech—"Let's not waste time"—waved his miners forward.

They filled the shaft and the tunnel, they thronged into the cave; when the Mink had shown them the machine to be moved, they fought one another for the honor of being first to touch it.

It stood solidly on the floor, ten feet high, twelve wide, square and black with twin coils and a thick projection like an enormous gun on the top. Men jammed around it, bent and gripped a ledge near the bottom, heaved up. Loath to move, it rocked a bit, then was hoisted off the ground. They staggered forward with it.

The hole in the wall was far too small.

"Miners! The best of you, and I don't want braggarts and second-raters, but the best! Tear down that wall!" Revel stood on a case and roared his commands. Men pushed out of the tunnel's throng, big bearded men, small tough men. They stood shoulder to shoulder and at a word began to swing their picks. Up and down, up and down, smite, smite, carve the rock away...

Soon they picked up the machine again, and manhandled it out into the tunnel. The crowd pressed back, and the Mink bellowed for the distant ones to go up the shaft to the top.

"How you going to get it up to the ground?" asked John. His voice had a kind of confidence in it, a respect for Revel that surprised the big miner. John evidently believed in him, was even relying on his mind when John himself was so overwhelmingly intelligent. Revel wondered: if he, the Mink, were to fall asleep and wake in a future time, knowing all his friends and relatives were dead long since, knowing his whole world had vanished...would he be as calm and alert and interested in things as John?

There was a man, by—what was the expression he used?—by god!

"We'll get it there," he said. "So long as you can work it, John, there aren't any worries."

"Understatement of the millenium, or is that the word I want? Optimistic crack o' the year. Okay, Revel. It's your baby."

Slowly the men carried the machine to the lip of the shaft. Nothingness yawned above for ninety feet, below for over a hundred. The shaft was twenty feet across. "Now what?" asked Lady Nirea.

"There's an ore bucket at the bottom; we toss our coal down the shaft, and once a day the bucket's drawn up to the top, by a hoisting mechanism worked by ten men, and the coal's emptied out and taken away in small loads. The bucket fills that shaft. It's two feet deep but so broad it holds plenty of coal. You can see the cable out there in the center; it's as tough as anything on earth."

"I see your idea," said John. "I *hope* that cable's tough. The machine weighs a couple of tons."

"Tons?"

"I mean it's heavy!"

Revel bawled for the men at the top to start the winch. Shortly they heard the creak and groan of the ore bucket, coming slowly toward their level. When its rim was just level with the floor of the tunnel, the Mink let go a yell that halted the men on the windlass like a pickax blow in the belly; then Revel said, "All right, move it onto the bucket!"

"For God's sake, be careful of it," said John. "That's a delicate thing." He leaped down into the huge bucket. "Take it easy," he cautioned the miners, straining and sweating at the work. "Easy…easy…easy!"

The great square mysterious box thrust out over the lip, teetered there as if it would plunge into the bucket. John with a screech of anguish jumped forward and thrust at it with both hands.

If it fell now it would smash him to a pulp, and Revel's chance to drop the buttons from the sky would be gone forever. Nobody on earth could ever learn to manipulate such a complex thing as the *antiforcescreenthrower* of John.

The idiot had to be preserved. Revel dropped his pick and launched himself into space, lit unbalanced and fell against John, rolled over sideways pulling the amazed man from the past with him.

The machine teetered again, then a score of men were under it and lowering it gently into the bucket. The broad round metal container gave a lurch, then another as the machine settled onto its bottom. It tipped gradually over until it seemed to be wedging itself against the wall of the shaft. Revel howled, "Into the bucket, you lead-footed louts! Balance the weight of that thing, or the cable'll be frayed in half!"

Miners piled down, filling the bucket; it was hung simply by the cable through its center, and when coal was loaded into it the mineral had to be distributed evenly if the bucket was to rise. Now it slowly righted itself, came horizontal again.

"Up!" roared the Mink. Nothing happened. "More men on the winch!" Then in a moment they began to rise.

The other rebels swarmed up the ladder. Lady Nirea and Rack kept pace with the bucket, anxiously watching Revel and John.

At last the bucket halted. Its edge was even with the top of the shaft. All that remained was to hoist the machine out and drag it out into the night, below the shining buttons. Revel, leaping out and giving a hand to John, ordered each inch of progress; and finally the *antiforcescreenthrower* was all but out of the mine. Another ten feet would bring it clear.

Then the world shook around them with a noise like the grandfather of all thunderclaps, the earth rocked beneath their feet, and the Mink felt his eardrums crack and his nose begin to bleed.

CHAPTER FOURTEEN

The Mink he turns his blazing eyes
Up to the buttoned sky:
"This night I'll tear ye down from there
To see if gods can die!"

The gentry mass in stallioned ranks,
The priests have gone amuck;
The orbs and zanphs they now descend,
All-armed against the ruck!
—Ruck's Ballad of the Mink

John staggered to his feet. "Brother! Maybe I was wrong. That was an atomic city-buster if I ever heard one—and when the Tartarians were over here, I did. Maybe the coal isn't so important to your damned orbs after all." He went reeling to the open night. Revel and Nirea were beside him now. Off to the west beneath the lurid light of the globes' buttons rose another of the dark twin clouds.

"If they were trying to smack us, they could stand a refresher course in pin-pointing…let's get the thrower out here fast. Too many saucers directly above us for comfort."

"There went another quarter of Dolfya," said Rack. "What power they have!"

"You'll see their power come plummeting to earth if I can work the machine," said John urgently. "Bring it out!"

The miners hauled it out, a titanic job even when men pressed tight against men and uncounted hands lifted the great burden. John showed them where to put it on the rock shelf. "Hoist me up on top," he clipped. It was done. "Now watch."

Revel stared at the sky till his eyes began to ache. At last John shouted, "I'm ready, but listen—I see a lot of torches coming up the valley, and the men holding 'em are mounted!"

"Our rebels, likely," said Jerran.

"Send men to meet them," yelled Revel. "They might be gentry. Pickmen and those with guns. Fast!"

"Okay, son," said John then, "watch the buttons just over us."

All heads tilted. A strange clanking came from the great box, a beam of thick-looking purple light lanced upward from the gun-like projection on top and fingered out toward the buttons. "Be ready," called John from the top of the machine. "This'll nullify the diamond rays for a few minutes, but then the things will be able to rise again. Your men must go out and break into the buttons before the globes can get 'em up!"

Revel issued his orders quickly. The purple light had now touched a button, which wavered from its fixed position, then as the beam caught it fully, dropped like a flung stone. Hundreds of voices bellowed the rebels' joy. Half a hundred miners leaped off into the night to attack the fallen ship, which struck the earth some distance up the valley with a shattering crash.

Already the beam, more sure now as John's hands grew confident of their power, was flicking over other buttons. The least play of its purple glow on the under surface of an alien ship was sufficient to send it catapulting down. The other buttons were moving, sluggishly, then more swiftly, coming toward the valley; and John could be heard swearing in a strange foreign tongue as he wheeled his great gun around and around.

A ragged volley of shots broke out in the western end of the valley. Revel jerked his head up. "They *were* squires!" he said. "We've got to get up there to help our men!" Rack motioned to the miners behind him and went off into the gloom; Jerran shouted, "Some for the fallen globes! Some have to stay to—"

Revel made a long arm, picked him up by the scruff. "Little man, are you the Mink?"

Jerran struggled ineffectually. "No, damn it, no!"

"Then shut your mug till you're told to give orders!" Revel dropped him, and roared out, "Two hundred men— Jerran, count 'em off as they pass you—to the fallen buttons! Pickax the globes! Break the skull of every zanph! The rest of you, up to the top o' this hill—spread round in a ring that circles this ledge, and don't let a squire or enemy through! We've got to protect John!" He turned, gripped Lady Nirea's wrist urgently. "Have you quick eyes and hands, love?"

"Faster than most men's, save your own." Her slatey eyes glowed eerily in the buttons' light.

"Then up you go," he said, and hoisted her up by the waist until her hands clenched on the upper edge of John's machine. "Perhaps you can help him. I can't spare a man yet. Luck, Lady!" He set off toward the nearest button, tilted crazily with its rim in a cleft rock. At the western end of the valley more shots were echoing and yells rose thin and frightened. He wished he could be in several places at once but the wounded ships were the place for a slayer of gods tonight.

The bottom projection, dark blue and some fifty feet across, had been knocked open by the force of the fall. From the dark interior zanphs were crawling, a veritable army of the six-legged, snake-headed beasts. An occasional globe floated out, but moving slowly as if it were sick. Pickmen were axing them out of the air with yells of glee, as the zanphs milled, then spread out to attack.

He swept his weapon in a long looping arc that tore the head off one and maimed another as it leaped toward him. It was the first blow in a personal battle that seemed to last forever. When one batch of zanphs and globes had been disposed of, another lay a few yards further on, coming out of another ship and another and another, some ravening to kill, some weak and sick, desiring only to escape. After the ninth "saucer" as John called it, Revel gave up counting, and slew his way from button to button, gore of red and yellow spotting and splashing him, wounds multiplying in his legs and arms and chest, half the hair burnt off his head by the energy auras of angry orbs.

His force dwindled. Men died with throats torn out by zanphs, with eyes singed from the sockets by globe-radiation. Men stood numbed and useless, hypnotized into immobility. Men sat looking at spilling guts that fell from zanph-slashed bellies. But still the Mink slew on and on, a tall dark wild figure in the uncanny light of the still-flying airships of the alien globes...

John was bringing them down faster than ever, and Revel must needs split up his small force even more, sending miners to each wreck to catch as many entities as possible. Many spheres of gold managed to rise into the sky, where they found sanctuary in other saucers: some zanphs went scooting for shelter in the rocks and bushes, but most stayed to fight and die.

He yearned to check his forces back on the hill, those protecting John's machine, and the men who still fought the gunmen in the upper end of the valley. But he dared not take his encouraging presence from the miners here. A button came swooping to earth not three yards from him, spraying him with clods of dirt, unbalancing him by the shock; a zanph gained purchase on his shoulder and tore flesh and sinew and muscle so that his left arm lost much of its strength and cunning. He killed it with the pick handle and struggled on into a mob of the brutes, panting now and blinking blood from his eyes.

Of his original two hundred, less than seventy remained. Still he dared not draw any from the protective ring. Where were the rebels that Vorl and Sesker and the others had gone to rouse? Probably raiding mansions miles away. He should have told them...oh, well. Surely the concentration of noise and buttons and gods above the valley would bring them soon.

A moment's respite allowed him to look at the sky. It was lightening a little for the early dawn, and the buttons were less bold; most of them hovered near the horizon, only an occasional one bravely sailing in at a terrific speed to make a try at bombing the valley. John, perhaps with Nirea helping him, had managed to bring down every one so far. But John and Revel would run out of luck some time, as every man does; then John would miss, Revel's arm would fail, and they would all die.

Even as he lowered his head a gargantuan blast shook the world below him. He fell into a mob of zanphs, who were fortunately so demoralized by the explosion that they ignored him till he could gain his feet and begin to murder them once more. From the tail of his eye he saw a mushroom cloud lowering just beyond the hill; he flicked his gaze at the crest where his men had been stationed to guard the *antiforcescreenthrower*—no human form showed against the gray sky. The blast had hurled them to dust, together with every tree on the skyline.

Finally—the gods knew how long he had fought—he found with amazement that no more foes were in sight. The buttons that had fallen were all cleaned out. Zanphs lay thick in heaps and lines, emptied sacks of globes dotted the bloody grass. He listened for the sound of firing from the upper valley; yes, there were still isolated shots.

His forces there still held, then. He glanced again at the sky. No buttons in range. They were giving John a respite—or was it a trick? Revel's tired mind wondered if John and Nirea were dead, and the gods playing with him this way...

He felt himself, his head, arms, chest, legs. He had been burned a dozen times by energy auras, only his incredible animal quickness preserving him, giving him the power to dodge away at first touch of the burning and slay the golden globes. The zanph bites atop the thorn scratches and hound gashes were rapidly stiffening his whole torso, his left arm, his thick-thewed legs. But there were shots in the upper valley, and Revel the Mink was needed there.

Wearily he gathered his men—twenty-six of them now, all as tired as he—and trudged at a broken shuffling lope toward the light.

As he passed the rocks where the machine of John sat, he scanned it with blood-shot eyes. A score of miners, perhaps thirty at most, stood around it, and the man of the Ancient Kingdom sat on its surface, wiping his face with a white cloth. Lady Nirea stood up beside him and waved her hand as he passed. He swung his pick in a big arc to show he was still hale and hearty, though the effort cost him much.

Through his dulled brain now ran one thought, one hope. It was a chant, a prayer, a focus for his beaten spirit, for though he had won thus far, he was so death-weary that he could not conceive victory coming to him at the last.

Just let me meet Ewyo. Only let me meet Ewyo without his horse. Give me now one fair fight with Ewyo the Squire of Dolfya.

The first man he met was Rack, engaged in binding up a torn calf with strips of his shirt.

"How goes it?"

Rack turned the walleye toward him, as though he could see out of it. "We have eight or ten left. All their horses are dead or run away. We stayed them in hand-to-hand combat, but when they drew back and began to use their guns long-range, we lost heavily. Now we're dug in along that rise, and they seem to be waiting for more squires, or horses, or something. I think they have twenty or thirty left."

"Then we have thirty-five or so, and outnumbered them."

Rack let his good eye rest on his brother. "Your voice is the croak of a dying frog, Revel. You must have lost a quart of blood. Your men are like sticks and sacks and limp rag bundles. You call this force thirty-five *men*?"

"We are still men, Rack." His voice, croak though it was, rang strong and fierce. "I can plant this pick in any gnat's eye I desire. Now do you lead us to the battle front."

"Yes, Mink." Rack turned and hobbled forward. "One of the slugs has sliced half the tendons of this leg, I swear."

"That wound is in the fleshy part, and won't trouble you for a week. Is that a man?"

"That's Dawvys."

Revel started back, appalled. The man lying behind the rise was red and brown from short-cropped hair to waist, his back a mass of blood—sparkling crimson in the light of dawn, where it had freshly sprung leaks, and dirty mahogany color, where the scabs had dried and cracked and flaked. It was a back that should have belonged to a dead man; but Dawvys rolled over on it without a wince and grinned at his leader.

"Hallo, Revel, bless your soul," said the former servant. "I'm glad to see you alive."

"The same to you, Dawvys," said the Mink. "Did you have any trouble in that pit?"

"I went to sleep when the hounds had passed, and never awoke till your men found me tonight." He stretched and grunted with pain; then, "I think I shall live."

Revel looked cautiously over the rise. Some fifty yards down the valley the squires were grouped in a knot, their costumes gaudy in the early light. A few of them were looking toward him, but most watched the far end of the valley. They were looking, thought Revel, for reinforcements. Time might be short.

He scanned the terrain. Where the squires stood, the valley was narrow, scarcely more than sixty feet across. Above their knot, to Revel's left, was the open mouth of a mine; the opposite hillside was bare and rocky, without break. A familiar voice behind him said, "What's to do, Mink?"

"Greetings, Jerran. Why did you leave the machine?"

"Nothing doing there. The gods are sitting on the horizon. Have you a thought?"

"See that mine?" He pointed with his gory pick. "Isn't that the western entrance of the great mine of Rosk?"

Jerran took his bearings. "It is."

"Then the other entrance is back yonder, and through it we can traverse the mine and come out that hole-above the squires."

Jerran nodded. "The best plan under the circumstances. Let's go."

Rack said, "I come too."

"Yes, all of us save four men," agreed Revel. "They must stay here to create noise and pretend to be forty people. Give us ten minutes, and the squires will find that mine shaft erupting death all over them!"

CHAPTER FIFTEEN

The Mink has fought till nearly blind,
Till almost deaf and dumb;
Till all his strength is waned away,
And all his senses numb.

At last his foemen give before
His pick as swift as fire;
Before him now there stands alone
The cruel, and savage squire!
  —Ruck's Ballad of the Mink

With thirty men at his back, Revel went down the valley at a crouch; slipped up the rock shelf to the eastern entrance of the great mine of Rosk, protected from the gentry's view by a chance outcropping of shale, and went into the darkness. The tunnel he sought was on the second level. He dropped down the ladder, unhooked a blue lantern to guide his way, and followed the narrow tunnel west.

Behind him the pad-pad of his weary men lifted muffled echoes, and he tried to set such a pace as would take them swiftly to the hill above the squires, yet not tire them further nor wind them before the battle. In the intense gloom he distinguished another lantern far ahead. As he approached, it appeared to move toward him. Was someone carrying it?

He tensed himself and swung the pick a little; but when the priest hurled himself at the Mink, bearing him back against Jerran, the Mink was caught by surprise. It had been no lantern, but the priest's glowing robe!

Revel's reflexes were still, if not hair-trigger, at least very quick. This was a tough priest, though, a lean hardbitten man, with a fanatical long face that shoved itself into Revel's and clicked its teeth a quarter-inch short of his nose. The fellow's arms were tight about him, as they rolled sideways against the rock, Revel straining to bring his pick into play, clutching tight to the lantern, while the priest flailed hands like knobby boulders against the Mink's nape and head. A blow of his knee, and Revel doubled up, gasping; struck out blindly with the lantern, caught the fellow in the belly, and made him curl up in his turn, choking for breath. Jerran and the others were blocked by Revel, and growled encouragement.

Revel straightened, nauseated and weak. The priest came at him. Revel raised his pickax and swung it—pain stabbed into his legs and belly—he bent involuntarily in the middle of his swing—and what should have been a neat spitting of the holy man's skull became a messy job of disemboweling. The fellow died gurgling, picking futilely at his spilt entrails. Revel crawled over him and went on once more, his troops behind him.

At the western entrance to Rosk's mine, he peered out for the first sign of the highborn enemies. A thrill of panic touched him as he saw they were not where they had been; then, poking his head into the dawn, he saw them advancing in a slow line toward the rise where his four men were raising shouts and taunts.

Orbs, he thought exultantly, here's a piece of luck! We'll take them in the back!

He slipped down the shelf, gesturing his men on. Running silently, he came within a yard of a squire in green and gold; then halted and cleared his throat loudly. The squire, startled, looked back.

"Ewyo!" he shrieked, whirling. "It's the Mink!"

"Come from Hell to slay you," said Revel between his teeth, and dealt a blow with his pick that clove the gentryman from brow to breastbone. The line of men had swiveled, and now shots rang out; at such close range even their guns could not miss. Half a dozen rebels fell, screaming.

And now the weary Revel was a brazen-throated fiend, brandishing his pick, roaring, scalping one and braining the next, destroying with fresh vigor dredged up from the pits of his free soul. For now he had a strange certainty that the gods were done, and if he died in this moment he died emancipated.

Joy brought him strength such as he had never had. These squires, running off, loading their guns feverishly, firing, clubbing their weapons to stand and fight, what chance had they against him? He looked for Ewyo, but could not find him. *Let him not be dead*, he prayed. And then there was Rosk.

Rosk, red of visage, narrow of jaw, bloody about the thin mean mouth, facing him over a thrust-out gun. Revel jumped aside, but Rosk did not fire, only following him with the musket muzzle. "Don't bounce, Mink," he grated. "Stand and look around you. Your men are falling faster than autumn leaves."

Revel glanced behind, and at that instant Rosk fired. It was a treacherous trick, and by poetic justice it was his last. The ancient gun, overheated by long use, could not take the overcharge of powder in the shell. It blew up, its barrel twisting into twin spirals of metal, its stock driving back into the guts of the squire, fragments of hot iron spraying his face and chest. Rosk had no time to howl, but went down like a lightning-struck birch. Revel felt the slug, or a piece of the shattered gun, burn along his cheek.

What was one more wound atop the uncounted number he had? The Mink laughed, turning to his men.

Of the thirty, Rack and Jerran and one other remained. Each was engaged with a squire, his two friends grappling without weapons, the miner swinging a pick against a clubbed gun. All the others were dead or dying. Ewyo must be dead somewhere in the valley, or else he had not been here at all.

Revel hurried tiredly to the nearest combatants, let his pick go licking out over Jerran's small shoulder, tore off half the head of the squire. Rack crowed triumphantly as he throttled his man. The miner had won his fight. They were finished.

The four of them limped toward the hill of John's machine.

Then there came a pounding of hoofs on greensward behind them. Revel turned. It was a lone rider, galloping furiously down upon them. He saw, with an incredulous gasp, that it was Ewyo of Dolfya.

"Go on," he said urgently. "Leave me, comrades."

"You young *fool*," barked Jerran. But he took Rack's arm and pulled the giant forward, leaving Revel standing alone with his face toward Ewyo.

The stallion was pulled up short, and Ewyo stared down at him. "I hoped I would get here in time," he said.

"You're late. Your world is broken, Ewyo." Revel realized as he said it that he was fatigued to the point of not giving a damn whether he lived or not. Still there was a yearning to fight this devil on horseback. "Shoot, Ewyo. I shall kill you all the same."

Ewyo raised his gun, hesitated, then said, "Is there only myself, then, and you, Mink, in all the world?"

"In all the world, Ewyo."

"Will you give me a pick?"

Revel started. "You are no miner. You can't fight with a pickax."

"I can fight with anything I can hold." He threw the gun on the grass. "Give me a pick," he commanded, leaping from his nag.

Revel stooped and took up the weapon of a dead man. It was a good pick, with a longer handle than the Mink's own. He reached it out to Ewyo, holding it by the head, and the squire took it and stepped back a pace.

"When you're ready, Mink."

"Now, Ewyo."

They circled each other, warily watching the eyes and arms of the enemy. "Why didn't you shoot me?" asked Revel in wonder.

"Too unsporting," growled the beefy squire, his pale eyes squinting with strain. "A gentleman doesn't take advantages."

Revel laughed. It was too ridiculous a statement to merit an answer. He made a feint, Ewyo parried skillfully. Then the squire brought his pick down in a looping arc. His reach was as long as Revel's, and the pick gave him an advantage. Revel jumped back, slashed sideways and missed. They circled.

"The gods will win out," grunted Ewyo.

"Their day is done. We are aided by the Ancient Kingdom."

"Superstition! Things have always been as they are."

Slash, hack, parry and retreat. "Not as they are now, Squire Ewyo."

Ewyo dropped his guard, Revel came in to gut him. Too late he saw the trick, and Ewyo's pick sliced across his shin, a shallow cut that nicked the bone. He jabbed with the flat of the blade, struck Ewyo in the chest, and jerking his pick sidewise and back, tore velvet coat and satin weskit and drew blood. Ewyo cried out.

Revel summoned his strength and began a series of flashing swings, which Ewyo parried frantically, backing across the grass. Blood spurted from cheek and hand as the rebel's deadly weapon glinted dully in blurred movement before the squire's eyes.

Then the squire rallied, and his power being greater than Revel's now, if his skill were less, he drove the Mink back in turn.

There came a blow that turned the pick in Revel's hands, sending its point down to the side; Revel recovered, but the squire threw up his arm and brought down his blade with such force that the off-balance Mink could not turn it wholly. It sliced over his ribs, drove through the flesh of his hip.

Pain so hideous as to make him dizzy and ill knifed the Mink. In that moment he knew if he did not make one superb effort he was done. Conquering agony, he swung up the pick before Ewyo could recover from the vicious downswing. With a noise like a rock hurled into a rotten melon, the pick tore through cloth and flesh to lodge in Ewyo's belly, half its head buried in the screaming squire.

Ewyo tore it from the Mink's hands as he fell, and writhed about it, curled like a stricken serpent.

The Mink dropped to one knee beside him, head bowed with nausea and relief. "You were a brave man, you bastard."

Ewyo, strong in his fashion as Revel in his, stiffened his body so that he could look straight up at his killer. "Not—especially brave," he ground out. "You see—Mink—I had no—ammunition—for the gun…"

His pale eyes filmed over, and Revel staggered off, leaving him for the crows and worms of the valley.

When he had come, dragging himself like a wounded stag up the rock shelf, they stared at him in silence for a long minute. Lady Nirea at last said, "But you are dying, Revel!"

"Not for a good many years," he grinned.

Jerran said, "Aye, cut him a thousand times and he'll make fresh blood from that valiant heart!"

John called, "Look there, Mink!" Down the dawn wind rode half a dozen golden orbs, high enough to be out of reach of their picks, low enough to observe them. Revel gritted, "Blast 'em!"

"You can always shoot later, son. Let's hear what they want."

Reluctantly Revel waved a crimsoned hand to stop his gunmen. The globes halted a few feet above the machine. Fingers of thought pried into the Mink's head, and automatically up went his screen.

Then the cerebral prying ceased. John murmured, "They're talking to me."

Revel watched the silent exchange of thoughts. What if the obscene things got hold of John's mind. Anxiously he scanned the strong face for signs of fading will. At last he could stand it no longer, and was about to order a volley, when John said, "I think that's it, Mink."

"What happened?" they all asked eagerly.

"The things parleyed. They see they can't get close enough to smash the machine—that last explosion was a

202

desperate try at crashing a saucer with a bomb ready to trip, and it didn't work—so they want to talk. I gave 'em a skinful." He chuckled. "Told 'em there were men of my time wakening all over the world, with machines to defeat them totally; they know whom they're dealing with now, and they're going to talk it over. Mink, that's the end of the gods, with luck! They won't face a force of twenty-first century scientists. They haven't got it, they just haven't got it."

"But they'll discover that you lied," said Nirea. "They'll get the thrower, sooner or later, and then we're at their mercy again."

"I didn't lie, girl. All over this hemisphere there are caves like the one I came from, with scientists held in suspension, plenty of machines from our time, and knowledge that will bring your world out of these Dark Ages into another Renaissance! I have the locations in the papers that were interred in the casket under me, and we'll send parties out today to find 'em. This is a new world dawning this morning." He leaned over and kissed her enthusiastically, and Revel, who would have split another man down the brisket for that, did not mind at all. "Your globes are done, Mink. The gentry and the priests will be easy prey. You can probably scare them into surrender after last night."

Jerran said, "Here be men on horses, Mink." Revel turned and saw a great cavalcade of stallioned men sweep down the valley, and in a moment of great joy saw that they were all ruckers, carrying dead gods on pikes and singing the Ballad of the Mink as they came.

The Lady Nirea was in his arms, kissing his lips that were caked with three kinds of blood; and Revel the Mink forgot the pain in his torn body, the utter weariness of brain and muscle, and everything else except what was good and sweet and wonderful.

Three months had passed, and the leaders of the successful rebellion of Earth were sitting in a drinking-house (legal now) downing toasts to various people and events. Revel and his wife Nirea sat at the head of the board, and down the sides ranged their friends and lieutenants: the giant Rack and the tiny Jerran, Dawvys and a dozen others, with John Klapham at the foot.

"To the end of the globes," said John, his tongue a trifle thick by now. "By gad, you brew potent stuff in these times! To the gods' finish!"

They drank that standing, roaring it out gleefully.

Revel said, "It was a sight to see, that—thousands upon thousands of buttons, all sweeping into the sky and vanishing into dots and then nothing…and here's to the gentry they took with 'em!"

"How many went?" asked Nirea, though she knew as well as he.

"Seven thousand and four hundred and ten, squires and their ladies, electing to travel out of the world for promised power in another!" Revel grinned wolfishly. "And here's to the priests who weren't allowed to go, and so have become miners and know what it is to sweat!"

Rack stood up, looming gigantic above them. "Here's to the men awakening now all over this country—the men of the Ancient Kingdom!"

"And the things they can teach us," added Jerran.

"And a toast to the most important of those things— the art of tobacco growing!" shouted John gaily.

They sat down after that, and Revel said to John affectionately, "If it hadn't been for you, friend, we'd still be ruckers and worse. You gave us a new world."

"Rot. I gave you a technical skill—you furnished the brains, brawn and motivating force, a legend come to life. I was only one more weapon in your hand."

Lady Nirea touched the Mink's arm tenderly. "We'll all be weapons in your hands now, Revel. Tools to make a civilization again—to make the last verse of the old song come true."

"Let's sing it," said Dawvys, a little in his cups by now. "Let's all sing it loud."

"The gods have flown beyond the sky,
The priests toil underground;
The gentry's curse is lifted free,
And all our foes are downed...

"Now over all the Mink he reigns,
And gone are rank and caste;
The ruck is lifted from the mire—
And we are free at last!"

They finished the rousing song and looked expectantly at the Mink; but he had borne back Lady Nirea on the bench and was kissing her with enormous warmth, so that even a prophetic song, written about him ages before he was born, could not tear loose from him the only chains that would ever bind him again—the wrought-steel, invisible, shatter-proof shackles of Nirea's love.

THE END

If you've enjoyed this book, you will not want to miss these terrific titles...

ARMCHAIR SCI-FI & HORROR DOUBLE NOVELS, $12.95 each

D-11   **PERIL OF THE STARMEN** by Kris Neville
THE STRANGE INVASION by Murray Leinster

D-12   **THE STAR LORD** by Boyd Ellanby
CAPTIVES OF THE FLAME by Samuel R. Delaney

D-13   **MEN OF THE MORNING STAR** by Edmund Hamilton
PLANET FOR PLUNDER by Hal Clement and Sam Merwin, Jr.

D-14   **ICE CITY OF THE GORGON** by Chester S. Geier and Richard Shaver
WHEN THE WORLD TOTTERED by Lester Del Rey

D-15   **WORLDS WITHOUT END** by Clifford D. Simak
THE LAVENDER VINE OF DEATH by Don Wilcox

D-16   **SHADOW ON THE MOON** by Joe Gibson
ARMAGEDDON EARTH by Geoff St. Reynard

D-17   **THE GIRL WHO LOVED DEATH** by Paul W. Fairman
SLAVE PLANET by Laurence M. Janifer

D-18   **SECOND CHANCE** by J. F. Bone
MISSION TO A DISTANT STAR by Frank Belknap Long

D-19   **THE SYNDIC** by C. M. Kornbluth
FLIGHT TO FOREVER by Poul Anderson

D-20   **SOMEWHERE I'LL FIND YOU** by Milton Lesser
THE TIME ARMADA by Fox B. Holden

ARMCHAIR SCIENCE FICTION CLASSICS, $12.95 each

C-4   **CORPUS EARTHLING**
by Louis Charbonneau

C-5   **THE TIME DISSOLVER**
by Jerry Sohl

C-6   **WEST OF THE SUN**
by Edgar Pangborn

ARMCHAIR SCIENCE FICTION & HORROR GEMS SERIES, $12.95 each

G-1   **SCIENCE FICTION GEMS, Vol. One**
Isaac Asimov and others

G-2   **HORROR GEMS, Vol. One**
Carl Jacobi and others

If you've enjoyed this book, you will not want to miss these terrific titles…

ARMCHAIR SCI-FI, FANTASY, & HORROR DOUBLE NOVELS, $12.95 each

D-21 **EMPIRE OF EVIL** by Robert Arnette
THE SIGN OF THE TIGER by Alan E. Nourse & J. A. Meyer

D-22 **OPERATION SQUARE PEG** by Frank Belknap Long
ENCHANTRESS OF VENUS by Leigh Brackett

D-23 **THE LIFE WATCH** by Lester Del Rey
CREATURES OF THE ABYSS by Murray Leinster

D-24 **LEGION OF LAZARUS** by Edmond Hamilton
STAR HUNTER by Andre Norton

D-25 **EMPIRE OF WOMEN** by John Fletcher
ONE OF OUR CITIES IS MISSING by Irving Cox

D-26 **THE WRONG SIDE OF PARADISE** by Raymond F. Jones
THE INVOLUNTARY IMMORTALS by Rog Phillips

D-27 **EARTH QUARTER** by Damon Knight
ENVOY TO NEW WORLDS by Keith Laumer

D-28 **SLAVES TO THE METAL HORDE** by Milton Lesser
HUNTERS OUT OF TIME by Joseph E. Kelleam

D-29 **RX JUPITER SAVE US** by Ward Moore
BEWARE THE USURPERS by Geoff St. Reynard

D-30 **SECRET OF THE SERPENT** by Don Wilcox
CRUSADE ACROSS THE VOID by Dwight V. Swain

ARMCHAIR SCIENCE FICTION CLASSICS, $12.95 each

C-7 **THE SHAVER MYSTERY, pt. 1**
by Richard S. Shaver

C-8 **THE SHAVER MYSTERY, pt. 2**
by Richard S. Shaver

C-9 **MURDER IN SPACE** by David V. Reed
by David V. Reed

ARMCHAIR MASTERS OF SCIENCE FICTION SERIES, $16.95 each

M-3 **MASTERS OF SCIENCE FICTION, Vol. Three**
Robert Sheckley, "The Perfect Woman" and other tales

M-4 **MASTERS OF SCIENCE FICTION, Vol. Four**
Mack Reynolds, "Stowaway" and other tales

If you've enjoyed this book, you will not want to miss these terrific titles...

ARMCHAIR SCI-FI & HORROR DOUBLE NOVELS, $12.95 each

D-31 **A HOAX IN TIME** by Keith Laumer
        INSIDE EARTH by Poul Anderson

D-32 **TERROR STATION** by Dwight V. Swain
        THE WEAPON FROM ETERNITY by Dwight V. Swain

D-33 **THE SHIP FROM INFINITY** by Edmond Hamilton
        TAKEOFF by C. M. Kornbluth

D-34 **THE METAL DOOM** by David H. Keller
        TWELVE TIMES ZERO by Howard Browne

D-35 **HUNTERS OUT OF SPACE** by Joseph Kelleam
        INVASION FROM THE DEEP by Paul W. Fairman,

D-36 **THE BEES OF DEATH** by Robert Moore Williams
        A PLAGUE OF PYTHONS by Frederik Pohl

D-37 **THE LORDS OF QUARMALL** by Fritz Leiber and Harry Fischer
        BEACON TO ELSEWHERE by James H. Schmitz

D-38 **BEYOND PLUTO** by John S. Campbell
        ARTERY OF FIRE by Thomas N. Scortia

D-39 **SPECIAL DELIVERY** by Kris Neville
        NO TIME FOR TOFFEE by Charles F. Meyers

D-40 **RECALLED TO LIFE** by Robert Silverberg
        JUNGLE IN THE SKY by Milton Lesser

ARMCHAIR SCIENCE FICTION CLASSICS, $12.95 each

C-10 **MARS IS MY DESTINATION**
        by Frank Belknap Long

C-11 **SPACE PLAGUE**
        by George O. Smith

C-12 **SO SHALL YE REAP**
        by Rog Phillips

ARMCHAIR SCIENCE FICTION & HORROR GEMS SERIES, $12.95 each

G-3 **SCIENCE FICTION GEMS, Vol. Two**
       James Blish and others

G-4 **HORROR GEMS, Vol. Two**
       Joseph Payne Brennan and others